Startin...

I was still watching Marie climb the steps to the upper deck, when I heard whispered voices carried in the breeze. I couldn't place them, but I knew it was Tilde and Truman-Paul ... my children. Wherever they were, it wasn't the shuffleboard court.

"He's still looking at her," Truman, my nine-year-old, was saying.

"Men always watch women when they go away."

"How come?"

"Their butt," my precocious thirteen-year-old Tilde was explaining.

"Their butt?"

"I hope you don't get that way, Truman-Paul."

"Are you kidding: Why would I want to look at a butt?"

Also by Ron Renauld:

TIMES CHANGE
SAINT STREET
FADE TO BLACK
VISITING HOURS (as Kent Rambo)
PORKY'S
PORKY'S: THE NEXT DAY
SORCEROR'S BLOOD (as Ross Anton Coe)
TRAILS OF PERIL (as Ross Anton Coe

ATTENTION: SCHOOLS AND CORPORATIONS

PINNACLE Books are available at quantity discounts with bulk
purchases for educational, business or special promotional
use. For further details, please write to: SPECIAL SALES MANAGER,
Pinnacle Books, Inc., 1430 Broadway, New York, NY 10018.

WRITE FOR OUR FREE CATALOG
If there is a Pinnacle Book you want—and you cannot find it
locally—it is available from us simply by sending the title and
price plus 75¢ to cover mailing and handling costs to:

Pinnacle Books, Inc.
Reader Service Department
1430 Broadway
New York, NY 10018

Please allow 6 weeks for delivery.

_____Check here if you want to receive our catalog regularly.

TABLE FOR FIVE

Ron Renauld

based on the screenplay
by
David Seltzer

PINNACLE BOOKS NEW YORK

This is a work of fiction. All the characters and events portrayed in this book are fictional, and any resemblance to real people or incidents is purely coincidental.

TABLE FOR FIVE

Copyright © 1983 by CBS Theatrical Films

All rights reserved, including the right to reproduce this book or portions thereof in any form.

An original Pinnacle Books edition, published for the first time anywhere.

First printing, April, 1983

ISBN: 0-523-42062-5

Printed in the United States of America

PINNACLE BOOKS, INC.
1430 Broadway
New York, New York 10018

Pour mes Goobs,
with special thanks to Bob and Bert Renauld
and Jack and Colleen Miller, four of the finest
folks around.

TABLE
FOR FIVE

CHAPTER ONE

One of the first things I had done after giving up professional golf in favor of peddling real estate was to wrangle my way into a nice house on the beach. It had only taken me two months to land a beauty nestled between Malibu Colony and Paradise Cove. It was old and funky, a place with real character and a great view. On a clear day I could see San Pedro (and yes, I would sing that line in my worst Robert Goulet to any lady I could get a laugh out of with it), and when the tide was high, the ocean was at my back door.

On this particular day, it was slightly overcast, typical for June mornings in southern California. The waves were in great shape, and as I was packing I could see more than a dozen surfers out on their boards, waiting for a good one they could ride all the way ashore. Twenty years ago, I was one of those surfers. The Beach Boys were just starting out then and I liked to brag that I was hanging ten the day Brian Wilson showed up on the beach mumbling about this song he was writing called "Catch a Wave." Don't ask him, though, because I'm sure he wouldn't remember me. I was tall, tan and blond, like a half a million others frequenting the beach. I'm a little heavier now and I haven't touched a board in years, but I still look like I belong here. It was one of those things that made it easy for me to get what I wanted. In a town where surface appearances count so much, I learned early to cultivate the image of being "a natural."

I was kneeling on my suitcases to get them shut when Frank pulled his T-bird into the driveway and leaned on his horn. It's one of those trick ones that honks a tune, in this case that mating call from *Close Encounters*. Clever guy, eh? You bet. Frank was the senior partner at Malibu Realty. A real golf buff. He gave me my job after I helped him cut three strokes off his game.

Frank was into his second chorus on the horn by the time I made it to the doorway.

"Hey, Frank! Go ahead and park that, would you? We'll take my car."

"What for?"

"I don't want to waste your gas."

"Come off it, Tannen."

"I'm serious, Frank. Look, you have to come back this way, so we'll take my car and then you can bring it back. Come on, Frank, don't fight logic."

Frank took a deep breath behind the wheel. Brain exhaust. He was thinking about something. "Well, I was planning to drop by to see some folks at the Marina after I let you off."

"No problem."

Frank shook his head. "No, I'd really rather take the 'bird. Really, J.P."

Then it hit me. I glanced over at my old Mustang. I hadn't gotten around to replacing the crumpled front quarter panel. And the horn didn't even work, much less give off special effects. Hardly a machine to woo the Marina crowd with.

"Okay, suit yourself, Frank. I'll be right out with my things."

Besides the two suitcases, I had a bag for my camera equipment and a large sack filled with presents. Christmas in June. I took the sack and slung the camera bag over my shoulder, then surveyed the house, wondering what I was going to forget to bring this time. Last year it had been the plane tickets. I'd had a lot of fun living that one down.

I heard an ill-tuned engine backfire as another car came to a stop in front of the house. As I came back outside, a middle-aged Chicano man climbed out of a beat-up Rambler station wagon. Frank looked as if he were in fear of his life. I could see him picturing himself rolling in the surf with his throat slit while his stolen social security card was being used to create a new identity for an illegal alien. Frank was like that, a real trusting soul. I had to laugh at the sight of him.

"Buenos dias, Jesse!" I called out.

Jesse waved and tapped the brim of his hat as he smiled and came over to take my suitcases from me. Behind us, the other doors of the Rambler swung open and representatives from three generations of Jesse's family bounded out. Most of them were kids, yelling and screaming. I told Jesse that the rest of my things were in the middle of the living room. He barked a few quick orders to three of his sons and they ran into the house as the rest of the kids spread out to tour the yard. Jesse's wife and her mother walked shyly to his side and he put his arms around them. Frank took all this in with a look of increasing confusion. He breathed deeply again.

"Hey, come on, Frank." I told him. "You remember Jesse, don't you? This is his wife and family."

"Hi," Frank said stiffly, nodding at the newcomers. "Nice to meet you all . . ."

"Take a look at those kids," I beamed, watching them fall into a game of tag that quickly led down to the beach. "Aren't they great?"

"Yeah." Frank was still perplexed.

"Jesse's my cleaning man, Frank. You met him last fall when he was clearing the brush around the house."

"Oh, yeah. Right." Frank bobbed his head as it came to him. "Right. Gotcha."

The three sons emerged from the house carrying my suitcases. Their father helped them put them in the trunk.

"That's it," I said, "Next stop, LAX."

Frank looked back at the house. "Aren't you going to lock up?"

I shook my head. "Jesse's staying here with his family while I'm gone. Summer at the beach. They're gonna love it, don't you think?"

Frank looked at me strangely. He didn't even breathe. I went and got in my side of the T-bird, then rolled down the window to give Jesse some last-minute instructions. Frank finally slipped into the driver's seat and started up the car. Jesse turned his head and whistled, and the kids came running up to him until they were all gathered together and waving farewells, squinting their eyes against the sunlight that had started to burn off the morning fog. I waved back and reached for the steering wheel, as if to press the horn.

"Ta de dum dum da!" I sang out, impersonating Frank's horn as we pulled away. I was feeling great.

Traffic was thin and we made good time rolling down Pacific Coast Highway, passing the Malibu shops and making our way along the shoreline homes that Frank and I took turns staying on top of to see if the owners were thinking of selling. They didn't turn over all that fast, but when they did, you had to be quick if you wanted to get in on the sale. Handling the deal on just one of those beauts would bring me enough of a commission to replace the whole Mustang instead of bothering with color-matching the body work. I had other plans for that kind of income, though. Yes, sir, James P. Tannen was cleaning up his act. Making some big changes.

Frank must have been reading my mind.

"Real generous of you, J.P.," he told me skeptically.

"Jesse's a hard-working man." I had my arm out the window and drummed my fingers on the roof.

"Aren't we all?"

"What's that supposed to mean?"

"Just that you could have rented your place out for a few grand while you were gone."

It was my turn to take a deep breath and let it out slowly. "You're probably right. But would that make me happy. A few grand? Kids having a good time, that's what makes me happy."

"Christ, J.P., who's been spiking your water supply, anyway? Past few weeks you've been sounding like some cult freak. What's gotten into you, huh?"

I wasn't going to let him get to me. Things were going too smoothly. I glanced over at him. He was keeping his eyes on the road, but I could tell from his expression that his mood was slipping fast. Whatever he'd taken to get up this morning was wearing off.

"Can we just drop this, Frank? I felt like doing the guy a favor, okay? Listen, it's a hard life out there. These are hard times for people."

"You ought to know. You're into me for five g's."

"Oh, I get it. I should have rented out my place while I was gone so I could pay you back, right? That it? Look, Frank, you want it now? That what's eating you?"

Frank gunned the engine to beat the light at the Sunset turnoff. "No, I don't want it now," he snapped.

"Look, pull over and I'll get out my checkbook and write you a check," I shot back. "Right now. Okay? I'll write you a check for five big ones right this minute if you need it."

"Jesus, forget it, will you? I don't need it now and I don't want it now. Damn!" Frank reached over and turned on the radio. Somebody was in the middle of an aria. Caballe, I thought. Frank turned it back off before I could tell for sure. He wasn't finished with me yet. "I just wanted to make you aware that there are damn few people who owe money to practically everybody they know and then end up giving away their Malibu beach house to their goddamn cleaning man during the height of the high-rent season!"

I leaned back in my seat and pulled my hand from the roof when I felt a bug slap into it. "Well, I owe Jesse a few bucks, too." When I noticed Frank starting to grind his jaws, I put in a quick laugh and added, "Just kidding."

We slowed down for another light. Frank glanced over at me like he didn't think I was joking. I looked away, taking in the school kids mobbing the beach on this, their first week of summer vacation. Girls are looking younger every year, I swear. As we started moving, I drawled, "Listen, Frank. In three weeks, escrow closes on the medical building and you'll get your five back. Everybody'll get back what I owe them. Yeah, that's right. I owe a few people. I admit it, no big deal. I'm not ashamed. My cleaning man and his kids will have the best summer they ever had; so will me and my kids. Everybody's going to be happy. Good times are a'comin', Frank. Good times are on the way."

Frank shook his head and plucked a cigarette from his shirt pocket. He punched in the lighter and snapped the radio back on. The aria finished up. It was Sutherland, not Cabelle. I was wrong.

CHAPTER TWO

I was in the air by noon, and as Los Angeles fell away from view my thoughts turned to New York. It would be the big test for me. All the hassling from Frank and others was just a preliminary for what came next. I hoped I was ready. I didn't think I had much choice. All the planning had been completed and the course was set. Now I only had to convince *them* to take it.

Them.

I reached for my wallet and opened it. It was thick with everything but money.

My search attracted the attention of the young lady sitting next to me. She had a nice smile. One thing I like in a woman is a nice smile. Some other things are nice eyes, long hair, a good figure, wit, intelligence, humor and availability, not necessarily in that order.

"What are you doing?" she asked sweetly. Another thing I like in a woman is a sweet voice. So far so good.

"I've got a photo album stacked away in here somewhere," I told her, prying into secret folds of the wallet until I finally came up with a creased photograph. "Aha!"

She twittered lightly through her nose, still smiling as she leaned a little closer to me. "Private? Or can I see?"

"Sure, sure." I folded the photo the other way so she

could see. "Family portrait, minus me. It's from last
year's Christmas card, so it's really not up-to-date. You
know how kids shoot up when they're young. Take the
youngest one there. That's Truman-Paul. I called him
for his birthday last month and he told me, 'Dad, I've
grown another foot foot since I last saw you.' I told
him, 'Truman-Paul, I'm sorry to hear you grew another
foot, 'cause you're gonna look very strange with three
feet.' "

She kept smiling, but there was no laughter. Her
nose kept still. If we were at my place, I wouldn't be
launching into my Robert Goulet routine. She reached
over and tapped at the picture with a two-tone finger-
nail. "Is this your wife?"

"*Was*," I said. "We're divorced."

"Then this man must be . . ."

"Her husband. Right. That's Mitchell. A lawyer.
Nice guy." I had the photo folded so that half of him
was missing. I let her see the whole picture and chuckled, "Actually, I think he looks better with the crease."

She laughed through her nose again. Why do people
do that? Laughter should sound like you're having a
good time, not fighting a cold. "And who's this?"

"Trung."

"Tron? Like the movie?"

"No, Trung."

"Adopted?"

"Yeah."

"Viet Nam?"

I shook my head, still looking at Trung fondly. "I
met him in the Phillipines. He was a street kid. I think
he adopted *me*."

"How nice."

"He's great."

"A beautiful family."

"Yeah."

We were sitting in the two inside seats. An older
woman sitting by the window coughed and looked at us

with a trace of annoyance, the way librarians look at gum chewers. The younger woman patted her lightly on the arm. "Sorry, Mother."

"I was almost asleep, Sally," Mother grumbled. She didn't look anything like Sally.

"They'll be bringing snacks by soon. Don't you want anything?" Sally asked.

Mother waved the idea away and turned to look back out the window. We were somewhere over the Mojave Desert. The captain came on over the intercom to tell us we were making good time and that skies were clear over the Grand Canyon so we'd be in for a good view. Mother rallied at the news, and when the stewardesses made their way down the aisle peddling wares, she ordered one of those small bottles of Cuttysark to go with her soda and extra ration of peanuts. Sally took a Coke. I opted for two vodkas with ice. Somebody told me it helps fight jet lag. I think it was my bartender.

I had finished my first drink and was halfway through the second by the time we were over Grand Canyon. Sally's mother was hoarding the view, so Sally turned back to conversation. We spoke in whispers.

"What were you doing in the Phillipines?" she asked me.

"Winning a golf tournament. I was a golf pro. I met Trung out on the course. He was in the gallery the whole match, cheering me on. He was even cuter then and I couldn't help but love the guy, even when I found out he was rooting so hard because he had money riding on me. Eight years old and this guy had the street smarts of an old man. He was amazing. Still is, I'm sure."

Sally nodded. She was taking a closer look at me now. "Were you famous?"

I tried not to smile too wide. Liquor has a way of giving me a bad case of the grins. I get like that with Frank and he tells strangers this is my first time out since the lobotomy. "J.P. Tannen?" I told her. What more needed saying?

She looked out over her drink, trying to get the name to register. It didn't. She tried to hide her disappointment. "I'm not much on sports, I'm afraid. My mother-in-law golfs a lot, though. "As she turned and pried the other woman away from the window. I noticed for the first time that Sally was wearing a wedding ring. Oh, well, easy come, easy go.

"Mother," Sally asked the older woman, "Do you remember a golfer named J.P. Tannen?"

Mother shook her head. "No, does he play at the club?"

"That's alright, Mother, never mind."

Sally looked back at me and smiled shyly. "Sorry."

I finished off my drink and started thinking about a fair-sized colonial house tucked away in the tidy suburbs of Rye, New York, near the Connecticut border, where I had a family that would soon be getting ready to pick me up at the airport, filled with anticipation of my arrival.

CHAPTER THREE

The house is in turmoil as my kids get ready for their vacation with Dad.

I see four hands on the piano keys of a well-polished Steinway. Twenty fingers allied in spirited teamwork, filling the room with Mozart. My ex-wife, Kathleen, is on the left, with that lush brown hair of hers pulled up and away from her soft, gentle features. She's lovely. Maybe she's wearing the brown sweater I sent her for her birthday, but I wouldn't count on it. More likely it wasn't her style, like most the things I bought her when we were married. They say there's no accounting for taste, but you'd think after we were married as long as we were I'd have developed a sense of what suited her. No chance. Some are born color-blind; for me it was a broader affliction. Taste-blind. But no matter. However she's dressed, she's beautiful. A woman any man would be proud to call his own. How I let her get away from me I'll never understand . . . well, that's not entirely true. I know *how* it happened. *Why*, now that's another matter.

Tilde is sitting beside her mother and it's easy to see they share the same blood. Her real name is Matilda, as in "Waltzing Matilda." She was conceived on the fifth hole of the Royal Tartan Golf Course in Melbourne under the light of a full moon. Kathleen and I were on our honeymoon, and I had placed third in a tournament there, my best showing to date. I had birdied that fifth hole earlier in the afternoon, so it somehow seemed appropriate. So was her name, we thought. She had other ideas, though. Her classmates laughed at her during roll call the first day she went to school and she ran home crying. Truman-Paul was just a baby then and she locked herself in the bathroom, holding him hostage until we could come up with a nickname for her. Tilde it's been ever since. Now she's twelve . . . no, thirteen. A teenager. Her body's probably been doing strange and marvelous things to her since we were last together. Her mind no doubt is still years ahead of its time. She has the brains and the wits of the family, which can be a deadly combination. She can be charming and sweet when she wants to, but get on her wrong side and she goes from being precocious to insufferably bratty in the blink of an eye. My contribution to her gene pool, no doubt.

Kathleen's been giving Tilde piano lessons for a few years now, so I picture them handling the score before them with a delicate precision. When they reach the end of a page, one covers for the other while the page is turned and the music goes on without missing a beat. It's a picture of serenity and warmth, reinforced by the rest of the room.

Kathleen's always been one for surrounding herself with nice things. We had more than our share of fights when money was tight and I insisted that the first thing to cut back on was "touching up the house." I was always more ready to spend money on a weekend of good times than a new throwrug or some small antique Kathleen had spotted in one of the stores during the week. Now she doesn't have financial worries, and the whole house, basement to attic, is a personal statement. Not that my place isn't, too. But, as I've said, old and

funky is fine with me. I'm not into auditioning for
Architectural Digest.

Enter Truman-Paul and Mitchell, probably upstairs
dealing with the matter at hand, packing, raising their
voices to be heard above the tinkling of the piano.
Hello, reality.

"Is someone going to feed my fish while we're gone?"
Truman-Paul cries out in his high, nine-year-old voice.
It'll be a few years before puberty makes him crackle
when he talks. He looks more like me than his mother,
but he's on the shy side.

Mitchell is in the upstairs bathroom, going through
the medicine cabinet to see what they have that he can
pack and cross off a checklist he probably clipped out of
a newspaper feature on travel tips years ago. He probably had his secretary laminate the list so it wouldn't go
yellow and crumbly with age. That's Mitchell for you.
Master of details. Mr. Self-Discipline. The Good Provider. Husband, father, and friend to those under his
roof. If I look like the archetypal overaged refuge from
the California surf, Mitchell reeks of Ivy League, tradi-
tion, and well-groomed success. By all rights I should
hate the man, but I can't. He might have taken my
family from me (well, let's be honest; I lost them mostly
by default and he came in as I was on my way out of
the picture), but he's cared for them, about them, as
much as they need and deserve.

I see Mitchell wandering out to the upstairs hallway
overlooking the living room, staring at a plastic bottle
with a look of consternation. If he doesn't have anything
in the other hand, he's probably scratching his beard.

"Does anyone know what DDK is?" he wonders aloud.

Hands still on the ivories, Tilde tells him, "It's for
diarrhea."

"This stuff is three years old."

"We've been healthy lately." Tilde glances up and sees
Mitchell smirking at her joke. She's pleased.

Truman-Paul comes out of his room, calling, "Mom?"

"Yes?" By now Kathleen sees that Tilde's last lesson of the summer is destined for an early end, but she continues to play. Tilde follows, but her concentration is suffering and she winces at a few missed notes.

Truman-Paul's at the stairway railing. I'm not sure how much he's grown, but last Christmas he had to stand on his tiptoes just to get his eyes and nose above the railing. With his big blue eyes he looked like Son of Kilroy. "Can you come watch how to feed my fish?" he pleads.

Tilde misses another note. Her smile's gone now. Horns are sprouting through her barrettes. She yells at her brother testily, "She's playing the piano right now, Truman-Paul. Can't you see?"

Mitchell shakes his head at the list before him. "How are we supposed to know what they're going to need? For all we know, they might need thermal underwear and harpoons." He gets like this every year. The thought of some matters being out of his control makes him crazy. It's probably one of the reasons I do it this way. I like to see him off the pedestal now and then, hanging out amongst us mere mortals.

Kathleen reaches the end of a passage and gently closes the book as she gets up from the piano bench. "I think we better get your things together now," She tells Tilde. To Truman-Paul, she calmly adds, "I'll be right up."

That's not soon enough for Truman-Paul if I know him. "That's okay. I don't care, *let* them starve. I don't care if all the fish I love die." He disappears into his room. Starting up the steps, Kathleen and Mitchell exchange a look that is universal among all parents. It's that look that unanimously declares that children can be totally impossible sometimes.

But there are still a few inhabitants under this roof who haven't been heard from yet. It's time that Rodessa, the maid, showed up. She's probably been off cleaning up the master bedroom . . . no, let's stay away from the bedroom. Some topics we don't discuss, and one of them is anything that goes on in the master bedroom. I heard Rodessa raising a holler in the kid's bathroom, her rich black voice echoing off the shower stalls.

"Hey, no! Will you get outta here, Julius? Get outta here!"

On cue, an old, faithful Golden Retriever scampers out of the bathroom and quickly bounds down the steps, almost bowling Kathleen over. Rodessa emerges, shaking a feather duster, visibly agitated. To anyone who will listen, she declares that Julius Caesar, spoiled mutt extraordinaire, has been drinking out of the toilet again.

Truman-Paul has finished throwing his fit, so I see him coming back out of his room, ready to vie for more attention. He meets his mother halfway up the steps, holding a handful of what looks like pregnant spaghetti.

"Lookit, Mom. These are Tubifex worms!"

Kathleen keeps on walking up the steps. She knows all about Truman-Paul's Tubifex worms and has no burning desire to "lookit" them. "Don't drop them on the rug, please."

Truman-Paul's not one to give up easily. He follows his mother, holding the worms up toward her with both hands. "I want you to smell 'em, 'cause you have to know what they smell like when they're dead."

"Would you please ask Mitchell to smell them?" Kathleen answers with a sigh.

Tilde is still downstairs, improvising on the piano, ever the diligent student. She looks up to the commotion on the second floor and asks her mother, "Would you like to hear me play the piece we practiced yesterday?"

"Tilde, I think you better get packed."

To which Rodessa complains, "Trung ain't even started yet. He's just sittin' in that room of his, 'plugged in.'"

"Trung!" Kathleen calls out, heading down the hallway for the last room. "Trung!"

Shaking her head, Rodessa wanders off down the stairs, muttering to herself, "Wonder he don't get electrocuted!"

Trung's room gives new meaning to the concept of mass media. Last Christmas when I visited, he showed me his arsenal of video games, radios, stereo equipment, television components and miniature pinball machines. And this was before the stuff had become such a trendy phenomena. Now he's fourteen and his big ambition in life is either to win some kind of Pac-Man championship or, if I have my way, to go gungho into electronics so he can come across some one-in-a-million discovery that will make him and the man who first adopted him stinking wealthy. For the time being, he's "exploring his options."

Kathleen walks into the room to find Trung entrenched before a television set he can't hear because of the Walkman headphones he's wearing and the blaring of the stereo and the bleeping of the portable Donkey Kong game he's fumbling with on his lap. He has long black hair and Oriental features. If I wanted someone to paint his portrait, I'd try to track down a reincarnated Paul Gaugin. He's a troublesome kid, but it's not all that hard to see that his heart's in the right place. He's going to turn out just fine.

"Trung!" Kathleen shouts a third time, finally getting his attention.

Trung pulls off his headphones and looks at Kathleen as if nothing is out of the ordinary. "Hmmm?"

"Pack! And I want to see clothes in your suitcases, not any of these monstrosities. Okay?"

Trung has a look of bland displeasure he saves for moments like this. Once Kathleen's safely out of the room, one of his games is going to end up wrapped in underwear and packed away for the trip. Trung is one sneaky bastard if you don't watch him.

And that's the whole household, full of merry chaos,

and all because of me. I'm sure the point isn't missed on Mitchell.

"You know," he tells Kathleen, for the fifth time in as many summers, "if we knew where they were going, we might know a little bit more about what to pack."

"I know," Kathleen responds patiently for the fifth time in as many summers, "I know."

"Not that I don't appreciate a surprise . . ." Uh huh. Sure, Mitchell.

Truman-Paul butts in, confronting Mitchell with his booty. "Will you smell these worms, Mitchell?"

Mitchell's too busy clearing up this business about the soon-to-arrive J.P. Tannen. His eyes are still on Kathleen. "You *are* going to insist before you turn them over . . ."

"Of course," Kathleen says, ever-patient, ever caught between the two men in her life (don't I wish).

"You do agree we have a right to know."

"Absolutely."

Mitchell finally catches a whiff of Truman-Paul's treasures and recoils. "What the hell . . ."

"Those are the dead ones," Junior Scientist Truman-Paul explains, hefting one hand upward, then the other. "These are the live ones."

Downstairs, it's time for a new crisis. The dog's been out of trouble for too long.

"Julius Ceasar's scratching the door!" It's Tilde spreading the news from the scene of the crime.

"Hit him!" Mitchell calls down.

"Don't hit him!" Truman-Paul counters.

"That's a new door, Truman-Paul," Mitchell observes, then shouts down to Tilde, "Let him out; *then* hit him!"

Truman-Paul makes a beeline for the stairs. "No, don't hit him!"

"Don't spill those worms on the rug!" Kathleen tells her son.

Okay, I'm taking liberties with Mitchell. He's not a dog beater. When he says "hit the dog" he's talking about a light thwack on the hindquarters. Just light enough to make sure Julius Caesar misses the point.

So now Mitchell and Kathleen, husband and wife, are alone together near the railing, enjoying a respite from the pandemonium. They love each other, love the kids. I guess I should allow them a kiss here, a chance to be poignant and sentimental.

"Just imagine," Kathleen is saying. "By this time tomorrow, we'll have this big old house to ourselves for the rest of the month. It'll seem empty, won't it?"

"We'll manage," Mitchell says, edging closer to her. "I'm sure we'll manage just fine."

"I wonder where he's taking them?"

"Who knows? Is there a shuttle going to the moon? It seems like he's tried just about everything else."

Oh no I haven't, Mitchell. There's a lot of things I haven't tried yet. Just wait, you'll see I'm full of all kinds of surprises.

I'm a changed man.

There're going to be some changes.

CHAPTER FOUR

I awoke, not unsurprisingly, with a headache. It was probably due to the alcohol, but the operatic fury coming through the headphones wasn't helping matters. I reached under my seat for the tote bag I'd stocked some aspirin in, anticipating this. A stewardess was chatting with a businessman a few rows up. I got her attention.

When the stewardess returned with my juice, I invited her outside for a breath of fresh air. She was a giggler and I'd managed to punch the button that set her off. Putting her hand over her mouth, she excused herself and hurried back to the cubicle where the goodies were kept. She got her fit under control, but started up again as she whispered something to the other stewardesses. I assumed she was extolling my wit to the others and noticed a couple of them staring my way with something that looked like interest. I shook my head to myself, cursing the Fates. The one time I'm on a plane with people waiting for me at the other end and I was about to be seduced by a pack of love-famished stewardesses. They were probably conspiring right this moment.

It was the old me thinking, that little cartoon devil standing on my shoulder and whispering in my ear to do things I might later regret. Well, I was through listening to him, so I turned the other way.

Sally and her mother-in-law were both dozing. I took a long look at Sally. I remembered a time when Kathleen was that age and sitting next to me on a plane bound from Australia for New York. The honeymoon was over, but only in a literal sense. We were still aching with love for each other and couldn't wait to get back to the new house we'd bought in Connecticut. With my winnings from the tournament, we figured we'd be able to have someone come in and landscape the whole yard so we wouldn't have to do it ourselves over the course of God knows how many months or years. We'd sketched out our plans on the back of a cocktail napkin, debating choices until we couldn't keep our eyes open any longer. The airlines had just come up with earphones back then, so we decided to try them out as we sat back to sleep. On a flash of sudden inspiration, I'd disconnected Kathleen's set and cupped my hands over the plug, which was nothing more than a pair of hollow tubes that carried broadcasts from the armrests to the ears. As I'd suspected, I could whisper into the tubes so Kathleen could hear me. I'd started talking dirty to her, mentioning all the things I had planned for us once we got back to our own bedroom and crawled into our own bed. . . . Counting the time I knew her before we were married, we spent more than sixteen years together. Measure up the pros against the cons and all but the last four were good ones. Hell, ball teams with that kind of a record get to play in the World Series.

So why had I come up so short-handed? I'd let it happen, that's why. I'd let things slip away from me because at the time it just didn't seem worth the effort to keep them. Too much maintenance, too much care, too much commitment. It all seemed to get in the way of the good times I was having on the golf circuit. My style was being cramped, and, goddamn it, I had an obligation to style. I was J.P. Tannen, dashing golf pro, would-be celebrity and man-about-town. Make that man-about-world. I was international, not the kind of guy to get bogged down with home life. When I found out Kathleen had picked herself up a lover to fill the emptiness in her life, I'd been secretly relieved. It not only eased my guilt over the affairs I'd had along the way; it also made bailing out all that much easier. One day I was the man of the house, the next, Mitchell had stepped in like a long reliever. They moved to Rye almost as quickly as I moved to California and suddenly it was a whole new ballgame.

I wondered if things could ever happen that swiftly again. . . .

It was early morning in New York when we touched down at JFK International. As the plane taxied into the unloading area, I gathered up my things, filled with that mixture of anticipation and anxiety you always get when you've traveled long distances to tackle a new, uncertain experience. Usually, I'm the one who hangs back in his seat and lets everyone else leave the plane first, but today was different. As soon as the light came on over our seats telling us it was alright to undo our seat belts, I was up on my feet. I glanced back at Sally and her mother-in-law, who had awakened only when the plane had begun its landing approach.

"Bye," I told them. Looking Sally in the eyes, I added, "Thanks for the memories." She laughed through her nose and nodded a farewell. Her mother-in-law waved.

The stewardesses were all gathered at the front of the plane. I tried to ignore them. Let 'em down hard and they get over you real quick, I always say. One of them caught my eye and mouthed, "Thanks for flying Air National. We hope you enjoyed your flight." She sounded like a wind-up doll, especially when she told the passenger behind me the same thing. What a trouper. She was taking it like a real pro.

I had managed to be the first one to the exit, and the stewardess who had brought me my juice told me, "Can't wait to get a breath of that fresh air, I see." (No mention about wanting to join me in getting it.)

"I've got family out there I haven't seen in seven months," I replied, surprised at my nervousness. *What was happening to me?* "I can't wait to see 'em."

"That's nice," she said, opening the doorway to let me out. "Nice having you aboard."

"Thanks. You people were great. First-class all the way." My wit had left me. I was red in the face for some reason and quickly departed down the accordion—ribbed tunnel leading to the terminal.

Ours had been a full-booked flight, so there was a mob waiting for us when I came out, all smiles, scanning faces and listening for my name. I didn't hear it. The smile faded as I waded through the sea of happy reunions, slowly realizing that mine had been put on hold. They weren't there. I moved on to the main waiting room, but still no luck. I checked the time. Right on schedule. Where were they?

My first reaction was anger, but a few minutes of pacing worked it off and I started to worry. I elbowed my way through the throng to the service desk, but there were no messages for me. A dull voice over the intercom periodically beckoned for someone or other to call home, but they weren't talking to me. I called anyway. Mitchell's voice gave me a recorded spiel and told me to leave a message after the beep.

"Beep beep," I muttered in lame Roadrunnerese, then hung up. Well, they were probably somewhere between here and there. You know how this New York traffic can be, Tannen. Like rush-hour in L.A., only with more rust and profanity. There was nothing to do but wait.

I had my luggage together twenty minutes later and they still hadn't shown up. I tried calling again and slammed the phone down on Mitchell's recording. Mitchell. I bet this was his doing. Probably let air out of the tires when no one was looking and pretended there was a flat. It was time to calm down, pour a little vodka over the nerves and get the smile back on my face.

After a quick drink at the airport bar, I checked the waiting room again, then retreated to the nearest restroom. I had a day's growth of beard to keep me busy for a few minutes. One of the arias I'd heard on the plane was still running through my head, so I sang while I shaved, conducting myself with the razor. The acoustics were excellent.

Out of the corner of my eye, I saw a small figure scurry into the room and make its way to the urinals. On a hunch, I set down my razor and went to check. Looking down the row of dividers separating the urinals, all I could see were pant cuffs and a pair of tiptoes.

"Truman-Paul?"

There was a flush, then the figure backed up into view and looked my way. "Dad!"

"T.P.!"

"Dad!"

I squatted down and he ran to me. He *had* grown, but not enough that I couldn't wisk him up by the armpits and give him a bear hug.

"Dad, your face!"

I was done shaving, but I still had lather all over my neck and chin.

"Look at you, T.P.," I said admiringly, grabbing a towel. "So big! My God, you're using the grown-up *urinals* now!"

Truman-Paul beamed, then tugged my arm. "Come on! Everybody's lookin' for you!"

Kathleen and Tilde were standing together in the waiting room looking the other way.

"I found him! I found him!" Truman-Paul whooped. He rushed over and I ran alongside him like a circus clown, wheeling my luggage behind me. I thought I had enough momentum built up to grab them both and swing them around in a merry circle, but something stopped me. I don't know what it was. Some emotional airbag that triggers open at the slightest provocation. I don't know. I slowed down and took a good look at them from arm's length. My imagination hadn't done them justice. I just stood there, speechless and awkward, knots in my throat and gut.

"Hi, Daddy," Tilde said tentatively, looking up at me shyly.

"Oh, Tilde, look at you." My voice was cracking. This wasn't supposed to happen. I was on the verge of tears. "A beauty. You went and turned into a beauty. Just like your mother."

I took a deep breath, bringing myself under control as I turned to Kathleen.

"Hello, Jamie," she said softly. The corners of her mouth were turned up slightly. Her skin looked soft and delicate. There was a peaceful self-assurance about her, but when I looked into her eyes I could detect those deep-hidden scars I'd left on her. In an instant, it seemed that the whole facade I'd been nurturing of late was crumbling, leaving me helpless before her. She was close enough to touch but the gulf between us seemed beyond crossing.

"Hello, Kathleen." The words spilled out timidly. This was all happening wrong. It was supposed to be different this time. I was a changed man. Couldn't she see it? Did she want to? The silence was crushing me. I had to forge on. I smiled at her, looked her over from head to toe. Then it registered. She was wearing the sweater I'd bought her for her birthday. Goddamn, Tannen, there's still hope! Don't blow it, boy! Get out there and follow-through! "You look great, too. Just great. God, I forgot how pretty you are. You're beautiful!"

She kept looking at me. Her smile turned up a little more, but I could see she was biting the inside of her lower lip.

"Does that make you uncomfortable?" I asked her.

She relaxed a little and shook her head. "No."

I exhaled and gave a short laugh. "I'm not uncomfortable either. Isn't that great?" I looked over at Tilde and Truman-Paul. "See that, kids? How easy it is to tell your mother she's beautiful?"

Tilde and Truman-Paul stared up at me with blank expressions. I was groping for the next move when a shout sounded from across the room, cutting through the din.

"Dad!"

It was Trung, racing from the magazine rack towards me. He'd grown the most of all the kids, and proved it by leaping up at me the way he did fifty pounds ago. We both ended up on the floor. He kept calling me "Dad" over and over again. Now this was the kind of greeting I had in mind. I wrestled Trung a while longer, laughing the anxiety out of my system. There were a dozen or so people waiting in chairs nearby, and they quickly moved away from us as if they thought a mugging was in progress.

I finally eased Trung away and we both got to our feet, brushing ourselves off. I had rug burns on my elbows. I felt great.

"Well, now that we're all acquainted . . ." I rubbed my hands together, ready for anything.

"Where are we going, Daddy?" Tilde asked.

"Yes, we're all dying to know." Kathleen was watching me with knowing eyes. It was her patented You're-Never-Going-To-Grow-Up-Are-You look. Maybe I *had* spent a little too much time on the rug with Trung.

"Can we go somewhere with horses?" Truman-Paul cried.

"Or with museums?" Tilde suggested.

"Yeah, well, I want to talk to your mother about that for a second." I took out my wallet and divvied out the few dollar bills I had on me. "Now why don't all you guys go busy yourselves a while, okay?"

Trung took his take and rushed over to the arcade next to the cafeteria, with Truman-Paul in close pursuit. Tilde looked warily at Kathleen and me, then walked off slowly. Smart young lady. She suspected something.

"So . . ." Kathleen said.

"Let's go grab a cup of coffee," I told her. "We have a lot to talk about."

As we walked off, I risked giving her an affectionate pat on the butt. Not a wise idea, except that it gave me a quick idea of where I stood with her. I didn't.

CHAPTER FIVE

"Egypt?"

I'd taken her by surprise, all right. "Yep."

She stared down at her coffee, willing her fingers not to start shaking. She was also probably trying to come up with something to say, something that would properly convey her disbelief. The best she could do was another round of "Egypt."

I leaned forward and glanced over her shoulder, where the kids were engrossed in the video offerings of the arcade. It was going to work out fine. I just had to reassure Kathleen, get her used to the idea and let her know this wasn't just something I'd schemed up while I was flying over the Mojave.

"I've got passports for everybody, new clothes for Tilde, new clothes for the boys, too. A couple real nice outfits. And we're going to get our shots on the boat." I sat back, feeling like I'd laid out a straight flush after having my bluff called in a poker game. "I've got it all covered."

"Egypt." Kathleen was locked in a mantra.

"And Athens, and Rome, on the biggest, best cruise ship in the Western World . . . and don't say 'Egypt' again."

27

"I don't know what else to say." That wasn't true. She'd just been stalling while she came up with a hefty list of objections. After a sip of coffee, she started in. "Can you afford this?"

"Hey," I held a hand out. Such foolish questions. "Do you know what a real estate agent's commission is on a ten-million-dollar sale? Two hundred thousand. That's what I've got in escrow, and that's just a start. Things have changed for me, Kathleen. Don't let anyone tell you money can't buy happiness, because it's made a lot of difference for me."

I paused on the excuse of finishing my coffee. I was waiting for some kind of response. She kept silent. I knew that tack. It was her way of trying to disagree without forcing an argument. It was supposed to be my cue to back down gracefully. Not this time, though. I was through with that role.

"Look, Kathleen. I've being doing a lot of thinking lately. You know what I've learned about myself? I'm a guy who's spent half his life running away from success. I know you might not believe that right off, because you and everybody else has gotten used to the idea of me being a loser—"

"James . . ."

"No, I'm not afraid of that word, because there were a few years back there when—"

"Could we stick to the subject of Egypt, please?" she interrupted softly. What passes for anger in Kathleen was rising up inside of her. I could deal with it. I had to.

"Same subject. It's all the same. It's all part of what I've been going through. A change, Kathleen. I'm through just taking. I have things to give to people. Things to give to my kids . . . things they can't get anywhere else. And I'm not trying to knock Mitchell. He's a hell of a guy." I was rushing things, I could tell. I had to be more roundabout, let her see the whole picture first. I asked her, "Did I tell you about my idea called 'Village Green'?"

She shook her head slightly, pursed her lips to form the word "no." I barely heard it. I didn't like the look in her eyes. I looked away and concentrated on "Village Green," the foundation I planned to build my new life on.

"It's huge, Kathleen. A housing development built entirely around a golf course, sort of like the ones in Palm Springs, but even better. Every backyard will have a view of the course, and maybe a putting green or something and enough trees to give them privacy. . . ."

Kathleen started to stand up. "Excuse me, I have to get Mitchell. He's out waiting in the car."

I reached out and pressed down on her shoulder. "He can wait a few minutes longer. . . ."

"I want him in on this, too," she said firmly.

"What for?"

"Because it affects him, too."

"I want to talk to *you*."

"If it's about taking the children. . . ."

"It's not about taking the children," I told her, just as firmly. I'd get around to that later. She sat back down and clasped her hands together, like a hanging judge on Monday morning. How was I ever going to break through that wall of ice to get to the woman I loved? It wasn't fair. "It's about me, Kathy." The cockiness was gone. I was ready to get on my knees if I had to. "I've changed."

The verdict came in. She spoke bitterly, without raising her voice. "You haven't changed. You say 'pass the sugar' and tell me you're taking the children to Egypt. That's typical. Typical. Can't you just for once in your life do something normal, James? I can't tell you how many things this reminds me of. I don't even know whether or not to believe a word you're saying."

I wanted to shout at the top of my lungs, throw the cream pitcher, reach out and slap her; anything to snap her out of her preconceptions. Didn't she see what she was doing to me? My throat felt like it was stuffed with cotton. It took everything in me not to explode. I had to stay calm. I had to let her know that I wasn't just slinging hot air and empty promises.

"I want to come back into their lives," I said simply. I leveled into her eyes with my own, daring her to find a trace of insincerity in them. "This cruise launches a new me, Kathleen. As far as the children are concerned. I know I've let you all down in the past, but I'm ready to make a comeback. I think I deserve a chance. That's what this is all about. Slow boat to China, that sort of thing. A chance for us all to get it together."

Kathleen was blinking back tears now, letting the hurt pour out of her. Hurt I'd put there a long time ago. Don't, Kathleen. Leave all that behind. There's no point in dragging it around. I thought all of this, but couldn't bring myself to say it. All I mumbled was, "I don't think any of you has ever seen the good side of me."

"Don't do this," she said, her voice strained. "To them, to me, to any of us. Don't make promises you can't keep. I know your intentions are good, but please don't get their hopes up by telling them you're coming back into their lives. What does that mean, anyway, 'making a comeback'? People just can't change their lives to suit your whims." It was my turn to be speechless. I just sat there, letting it sink in. She went on, "They love you the way they have you. Vacations. Phone calls on birthdays. You're a lovely man, Jamie, but they've learned not to rely on you. They're secure with the lives they lead. You take them to the Pyramids and let Mitchell take them to the dentist. You do the cruises, let him do the carpool. You'll both be doing what you do best."

There was no viciousness in the way she said it, but that didn't make it sting any less. I licked my lips, but couldn't think of anything to say. I was devastated.

She took a deep breath, a prelude to the bottom line. "Mitchell says you need our permission if you want to take them out of the country. I won't let him fight you on that. Go and have a wonderful time with them. But leave it at that." She paused, waiting for me to look at her. "Please respect how happy we are."

"I *have* changed, Kathleen." It came out like the cross between a whimper and a whine. The defendant couldn't believe he'd been found guilty. Where did he go for an appeal?

I saw Mitchell coming over with the kids. Kathleen's back was turned to him so he couldn't see her face. I pulled myself together. There was no way he was going to catch me down and ready to be kicked. I stood up, mustering nonchalance. Hand out for a friendly shake, I met his gaze with a grin.

"Hi, ya, Mitch. Good to see you. The kids and I are going to Egypt!"

CHAPTER SIX

By the time we reached the docks later that day, Mitchell had resigned himself to the idea, Kathleen had gotten used to it, and the kids were all filled with the heebie-jeebie gamut of emotions any kids worth their salt get on the verge of vacations to new and strange places. I was in high spirits. After a shaky start, things were starting to go my way. In ways the kids had no way of understanding, I had an enthusiasm that even they would have difficulty topping. For them, this was the start of a three-week cruise. For me, it was the start of a whole new life.

I carried Truman-Paul on my shoulders as we threaded our way through the crowd on the docks, making our way slowly to the long walkway leading up to the ship. What a ship it was. I hadn't been exaggerating to Kathleen. It was right in league with the Queen Mary, they'd told me when I'd booked the tour. The ship dwarfed most of its counterparts in the harbor. Truman-Paul couldn't believe we were actually going onto something that size. As we started up the plank and I let him down to walk, he whispered something in my ear. I couldn't help but laugh. Mussing his hair, I turned to the others and pointed up at the rows of lifeboats hanging like strung baubles along the upper railings of the promenade deck. "Truman-Paul thought we were going to cross the ocean in those!" Lest he think I was making fun of him, I leaned over, kissing him on top of the head. "You are one crack-up. T.P. I love you!"

Kathleen and Mitchell came aboard with us, keeping close together and watching us with mixed emotions. It usually worked out that way, and was probably one of the reasons I'd always been wary about staying with them whenever I visited the kids. In a way, it gave me the feeling I was trapped between two camps, shunned by the grownups and feeling self-conscious about being clumped in with the kids, especially when Kathleen's favorite peeve had always been my so-called childishness. I tried not to think about it too much. In a few hours I wouldn't have to bother with it at all.

It was a Norwegian liner, so there was a steady undercurrent of foreign language being slung around as we made our way to the main deck and started down the welcome line, passing in front of the ship's crew. Somewhere inside the ship a band was playing European folk songs. Balloons were being inflated and passed around, along with streamers and small bags of confetti. The air rang with pending celebration.

I carried Truman-Paul as we met crew members, one by one, finally reaching the captain, a tall man with silvery hair and polished bearing. He introduced himself and I let Truman-Paul down to shake the man's hand. "Captain, I'm James Tannen, and these are my children; Trung, Tilde and Truman-Paul." He bowed his head with a courteous smile at each one of them. A few spaces back in line, I heard Mitchell doing his own introductions, calling the kids *his*, too. It came out naturally, and he didn't know I'd overheard him. Kathleen was looking at me, though. She'd retreated back to her attitude of polite discretion. Her face said nothing.

While Trung and Tilde gawked, taking it all in with greedy eyes, Truman-Paul strayed from my side. One second I realized he was gone, the next I heard him shouting from the sight of his big find.

"Hey, look! Elevators on a boat!"

When the elevator opened and the ship's navigator looked down at him with a black patch over one eye, Truman-Paul's smile capsized. He turned heel and ran to me for protection. To me, not Mitchell. Thanks, Truman-Paul. I needed that.

We joined up with the porter handling our luggage and followed him through the inside hallways linking the guestrooms. Except for the smell of the sea and the glimpse of an occasional porthole, it looked like we could have been on our way to hotel rooms. The kids hadn't run out of questions or commentary yet. They never do.

"Is this the back or the front?" Trung wanted to know.

"Are we under water now?" Truman-Paul asked.

Trung smirked. "It's not a submarine, stupid."

"None of it's underwater, Truman," Tilde told him, always ready to inform.

Trung peered into an opened door. "Is there a game room here?"

"They've got everything here," I assured him. "Pools, movie theatre, all kinds of stuff. And loads of kids."

I'd spoken too soon, though. As the porter stopped his cart and pointed out our rooms, a woman wearing the ship's colors wriggled past Mitchell and sashayed up to me. She wore a wild perm and the look of a true space cadet. Her smile was big and inviting. So were a few other parts of her.

"Mr. Tannen? I'm Mandy, the Children's Activities Director. That is to say, your children's activities director. It appears they're the only children aboard." I saw Kathleen's eyes widen when she heard this. Mitchell's lips tightened and he shook his head. I was living up to his dour expectations, as usual. I couldn't believe my stupidity in assuming there'd be other kids aboard. What was that Kathleen had said? Typical Tannen move.

Mandy left some brochures and strolled off as the ship let out a blare of its foghorn.

"Do they have headlights?" Truman-Paul asked me.

I let out a nervous laugh. "What do you mean?"

"How do they see at night?"

"There's nothing to see at night, Truman."

"Uh huh. Icebergs."

Trung snickered, "There's no icebergs in Egypt, stupid."

"Hey!" I turned on Trung angrily. Kathleen and Mitchell were behind him, waiting to see how I'd handle him. "Don't talk to him like that, Trung. It's not nice." I didn't bother to check for Kathleen and Mitchell's approval. Together, they were getting on my nerves.

"It's hot in Egypt," Trung defended himself.

Tilde assured Truman, "They have radar. It's perfectly safe."

"Then why do they have 'Emergency Exits?' "

I stepped in and started pointing out our rooms. "Okay, the boys bunk here. I'll take the middle, and Tilde, you're on the end."

Mitchell cleared his throat and moved in on me. "Uh, Jim? Could I speak to you a minute? Alone?"

I shrugged my shoulders. As we passed by Trung, he pointed out a sign on the wall, reading "LIVBAT." "What does that mean?" he asked me.

"I think it's Norwegian for 'Love Boat'."

"Maybe it means 'live bait'!" Trung said with a burst of excitement. "For fishing!"

Our porter deadpanned, "It means 'life boat.' There will be a drill as soon as we leave port."

"Life boat!" Truman-Paul gasped.

"It's just for safety, Truman," Tilde said.

"Don't worry, Truman," Kathleen said. To Mitchell and I, she added, "I'll help Tilde get organized."

I followed Mitchell into my room. It was roomier

than I'd expected. There was a bottle of complimentary champagne on the dresser, already immersed in a bucket of ice. I was ready for a glass, but held back from filling one. Mitchell thinks I drink too much. He can't handle his liquor and assumes everyone else has his level of tolerance.

"Jim, I think it'd be a good idea if Tilde and Truman-Paul bunk together."

"Oh? Really."

"The boys rub each other the wrong way."

"Ah, they'll be fine." I couldn't believe he was pulling this crap on me. Patience, J.P., I kept telling myself.

"There's a little more to it."

"Look, if they aren't comfortable, they can always—"

"Truman's kind of sensitive about this, but he has nightmares at night. Tilde's very good at handling it. She likes to look after him."

I thought it over, then waved his suggestion away. "Truman won't have nightmares here. He'll be fine. Besides, boys like to stick together."

Mitchell was about to become more insistent when Truman-Paul appeared in the doorway. He asked me, "Is it okay if I bunk with Tilde?"

What was this, a conspiracy? I looked down at Truman-Paul. "Sure." For Mitchell's benefit, I added, "That's all it takes. I'm not rigid. Tilde, Trung. Switch rooms."

Next door, Trung complained, "I got all my stuff in here."

"So, switch it!"

One thing about Trung. He's always had a snotty streak, even before puberty. I wanted to put a cap on it.

"I already put everything in drawers," he muttered.

"Well, take it *out* of the drawers . . ."

Trung mumbled under his breath as Truman-Paul and I came into the room. He sneered at Truman, "What a baby!"

"I am not!" Truman-Paul snapped back.

I stepped between them and glared at Trung. "Wait a second now. Was that necessary?"

Trung crossed his arms defiantly. "He's just afraid of the dark."

"He's not afraid of the dark, Trung."

"I *am* afraid of the dark," Truman-Paul said. "But I'm not a baby."

"Good enough," I said. I looked back at Trung and gestured with my thumb out the door. "Now move your ass, Trung."

"*I'll* move," Truman-Paul said, grabbing for his things.

"I told Trung to move."

"*I'll* move!" Truman-Paul insisted.

I threw up my hands. "Fine, fine. End of crisis, okay? Let's all be a little more civil the rest of the trip, all right? Come on, Truman, I'll give you a hand." I picked up a large blue duffle bag of his. It was heavy. "Jesus, Truman, what do you have in here? Bricks?"

We were back out in the hallway. The others were watching us peculiarly. I didn't get it.

"They're for reading," Truman-Paul whispered. I barely heard him.

"Books?" I held the bag up proudly. "That's great. You're a bookworm, huh? Fantastic. A whole bag full of books. You must be a real brain!"

The foghorn blared again, then the intercom came on, passing along a message in German, then Swedish. The kids looked to one another uncertainly. Kathleen and Mitchell had their eyes on me. I was saved by a drone of English pouring out of the nearby speakers.

"We request that all visitors leave the ship now. Thank you."

Kathleen and Mitchell both crouched down, gathering the kids around them, exchanging farewells, hugs and kisses. Misty eyes all around. I stood by watching, feeling apart from them, an outsider. It was the kind of feeling I'd arranged this whole adventure in hopes of getting rid of. The message over the intercom repeated. Kathleen and Mitchell stood up, keeping the kids between us.

"Well, I hope you all have a nice trip," Kathleen told me. "Take care of them."

"I will," I said. My feet wouldn't move. "I will," I said again. "Bye."

"Goodbye," she said. Looking down at the children, her voice quavered slightly. "I'm going to miss you."

"We'll miss you, too, Mom!"

"You, too, Mitchell!"

Mitchell smiled down on them. "Enjoy yourselves. Make sure your father looks after you."

He was looking at them, but I knew who he was talking to. There had been a number of times over the years when I wanted nothing better than to catch him in a dark alley, face to face with no one else around, and pay him back for all the subtle little digs he managed to throw into our times together. I owed him another one now.

Kathleen and Mitchell turned and fell in with the other visitors making their way back to the docks. We finished getting our things in our rooms, then joined the rest of the guests out on the deck for the bon voyage. We managed to spot Kathleen down on the docks, waving heartily, tears in her eyes. Mitchell was a ways away, standing in front of their parked car, with Julius Caesar perched precariously on the roof, barking. We all shouted until our throats were sore and our eyes were red from crying or holding back our tears. Balloons and confetti filled the air and drifted downward. The foghorn blew, sounding ten times as loud as it did when we were down below. The mooring lines were drawn away, and we set out.

Kathleen stayed in the front of the mob lining the docks, waving and waving, mouthing words that were lost in the din. I hoped she was saying "I love you" and I hoped that, since she was away from Mitchell's side, she was saying it to me.

CHAPTER SEVEN

And so we were off.

On the way back to our cabins, I saw that all three of the kids were feeling miserable. A natural enough reaction. I'd been through it with them before and knew they'd get over it once the farewell sentiments faded and their curiosity crept back to the foreground. I also thought it was important to get them quickly on my side. There was a lot I wanted to accomplish this trip, and most of it hinged on winning them over from the start, making a good impression upon which I could build the kind of relationship I was looking for with them.

I opted for bribery.

On our way to the promenade deck for the bon voyage ceremonies, I'd taken aside our porter and slipped him a five-spot to go back to our rooms and set out presents on each of the kid's beds. They were the outfits I'd bought back in Los Angeles at a shop in Marina Del Ray. I'd shown the sales lady the pictures in the wallet and left the rest to her judgment. She'd ended up picking out the same things I would have, so I was reassured.

"Okay, gang," I said as we came up on the rooms. "Let's all slip into something appropriate and meet back out here in ten minutes and take a little tour of the ship. How about that, okay?"

"Okay."

"Sure thing."

"Whatever you say, Dad." All this said with the enthusiasm of convicts being asked if they were ready to get cracking in the rock yard.

"Come on, you deadheads. Let's show a little enthusiasm here, what do you say?" I rubbed my hands together excitedly, then looked up and down the hallway to make sure no one else was about. Turning up my collar, I hunched over and did an impersonation that probably ended up being two parts Peter Lorre and one part Johnny Carson doing Lorre in a bad skit on the "Tonight Show." "Vee are embarked oopon a veeeery bick expedishion to deestahnt lands; lands zat are cloaked in zee deepest, darkest mestery. Who knows vat vonderful sangs lie in store for us, eh?" I raised my eyebrows suggestively, then left them laughing and slipped into my room.

I was ready for that glass of champagne now. It wasn't the best I'd ever tasted by any stretch of the imagination, but it was cold and left a fresh aftertaste after I'd downed it. I poured another one and sipped it more slowly while I changed. I'd splurged on a few new threads for myself, and after I inspected myself in the full-length mirror behind my door, I raised the champagne glass and toasted myself.

"To new beginnings." Glub, glub, aaaahhhh. . . .

Back out in the hallway, I knocked on the kids' doors. "All hands to the mizzenmast! All feet on deck! Attention! At–ten–shion! Zee exploration of zee ship vill be starting right pronto, jah!"

Trung came out first. Instead of the navy blazer and white slacks I'd bought to go with his Izod shirt, he was wearing the same jeans and t-shirt he'd had on all day.

"Hey. Where's your jacket?" I demanded.

"What jacket?" Trung Tannen's first rule of defense in the face of accusation: deny everything.

"You didn't open the box?"

"Oh, *that* jacket.

"Yeah, *that* jacket." He didn't look like he was about to go put it on. "What gives? Didn't you like it?"

"I don't wear jackets."

"It's a nice jacket. Did you try it on?"

He held his ground. "I don't wear 'em."

"Well, it's a rule on the ship. For dinner."

"What?"

"If you want to eat in the dining room, you've got to wear a jacket."

"Do I have to eat in the dining room?"

"Yes, you have to eat in the dining room," I raised my voice. "Now quit giving me a hard time and go—"

"I'm ready," Tilde interrupted, stepping out from her room behind us. I wheeled around and saw her fitting a ribbon around the band holding her ponytail in place. She looked wonderful in a party dress with matching shoes. Unfortunately, it wasn't the dress I'd bought her.

"Hey, you look great!" Harassment hadn't worked on Trung. I decided to try the flattery approach.

"Thank you," Tilde said, smiling as I helped tie the ribbon in her hair.

"Did you open the boxes?"

"Boxes?"

Tilde's a worse liar than Trung. "The dresses, Tilde."

"Oh, the dresses. I . . . I thought I'd save them. You know, a momento."

"Oh yeah?" I said. "Well, let's just *wait* a momento, okay? I would appreciate a little honesty around here. "Now, if you don't like the dresses, Tilde, and if—"

"I *do* like them," Tilde cut in. "They're great!"

I shook my head. "Look, if you don't like them—"

"I *do* like them."

"I don't," Trung grumbled, interrupting.

"Wonderful," I groaned. "Absolutely wonderful." I

wasn't handling this right at all. I went back to my
theatrics. Now I was Captain Bligh. " 'Still in sight of land
and the first rumblings of mutiny swept across the
crew. They refused to don their uniforms. What next, I
wondered with grim trepidation. Would they shun the
flag? Would they fail to raise their arms if we were
beset by pirates? Ah, it's a hard lot for a captain, mark
my words, lad . . .' "

Tilde giggled slightly and Trung buried a smile in his
fist, pretending to cough. Truman-Paul stepped out,
wearing a white sailor boy's outfit, complete with cap.
He was brimming with joy. "This is great, Dad! Thanks!"

Trying to hold my smile back, I clicked my heels and
saluted Truman-Paul. He stood upright and put his
palm to his forehead. It looked more like he was check-
ing for a fever than saluting, but he was so goddamn
cute I couldn't help stepping forward and tugging his
cap so it came down over his eyes, then lifting him up.
"Alright! One for three. That's good enough for me." I
set him back down and eyed Tilde and Trung with
mock gravity. "Ye won't be walkin' the plank this time,
swabs, but ye best be on yer best behavior, hear?"

Laughing, both Tilde and Trung offered up salutes.

"Yes, sir!" Trung threw in.

"That's 'Yes, sir, Dad' to you, Private Trung."

"Hey, man, I don't wanna be a lousy private."

"Then put on your jacket."

I'd pushed my luck too far. He shrugged his shoulders. "Hell, private's good enough, I guess."

"Onward, then!"

We were on board a small floating city, and it was
going to take more than a casual stroll to take everything
in. But, then, we had a long haul across the Atlantic,
plenty of time. I took them on the tour of essential
places, like where the bathrooms were on every deck,
and the clocks and where the staff hung out. Tilde
wanted to see the theatre on the veranda deck. Trung
wanted to see the bar. Before I could hand him a line

about there not being one, he pointed it out on a diagram of the ship. It was right next to the theatre, as it turned out. We went and watched a cartoon short, then stopped at the bar for drinks. I had more champagne, and the kids had Cokes. Trung, who usually has the posture of a slug, sat upright and used good grammar when he talked. I remembered trying to get served in a bar once when I was sixteen, so I knew what he was up to and told him to forget about it.

On the way out to the lido deck and swimming pool, we stopped off at the casino. The kids bypassed the video games and crowded together near a row of slot machines. I cashed in a five-dollar bill and passed around quarters.

"Okay, look, guys. I don't mind you playing these things, but don't get carried away with them, okay? Gambling's not a good thing to get yourself hooked on. Play a little, play for fun, that's the right philosophy." Of course, after I lost seven straight bucks on one of the machines without a win, I was ready to kick it in. Then I heard bells and buzzers behind me and turned to see Truman-Paul staring wide-eyed at a steady stream of nickels dropping like diarrhea from the bandit he'd been playing.

"Truman-Paul! All right!" I came over and plucked his cap over his head and set it under the coin drop slot to catch the downpour. "It looks like you're set for the rest of the trip!"

We all stayed in good spirits the rest of the morning. Walking together in a group, they'd listen intently as I explained the various workings of the ship. It was a good feeling and I wondered why it had taken me so long to come to my senses about dealing with them. This wasn't like other vacations, when there were long gaps of uncomfortable silences between activities I'd lined up to keep us all distracted until I thought I'd fulfilled my parental duties for one year. They were acting pretty much the same as they always had, asking a lot of questions and pointing out things for me to look at, but I was responding to it all with a better frame of mind. I was paying attention to them, letting myself become involved with the moment instead of merely tolerating it while my thoughts were elsewhere. I *had* changed after all!

". . . and, you see, the great thing about sailing is your chart your course by the stars."

We were on our way up to the bridge. A stiff wind was blowing across the sea, rousing the waves and giving the ship a slight sway. But nobody showed any signs of becoming seasick. As we entered the bridge, I continued, letting sentiment creep into my voice. "That's one thing that never changes. East is East and West is West . . . and a man is never lost if he keeps his eyes on the stars."

The room was filled with modern, state-of-the-art equipment, manned by crew members we had seen earlier, including the Captain. He'd overheard my remarks and strolled over to burst the bubble with a simple wave that took in one whole wall of the bridge.

"We use computers and satellite control these days," he told the kids. "We really don't have much need for the stars. See? We have radar in case we're too near another ship, depth finders in case we're too shallow, hydraulic stabilizers in case we start to rock, and satellite monitoring in case we stray off course."

"Wow!" Truman-Paul said, impressed. Trung grinned at me, and I got a teasing wink from Tilde.

"You don't need the stars?" I asked the Captain feebly.

"Only for romance."

"Well, that counts for something."

"What do we have in case we sink?" Truman-Paul was back to his favorite subject.

"Lifeboats," the Captain said. "Come. In a few minutes we will be having a drill." He motioned for the children to follow him. I stayed behind a moment, taking advantage of the view down at the swimming

pool. It was warm enough for sunbathing, despite the
wind and there were a lot of bodies stretched out on
towels and lounge chairs.

"Only for romance," I muttered, half-aloud.

"Yah," the navigator replied nearby. He was looking
down at the pool, too.

"Speaking of romance, how are we fixed for single
women aboard this ship, eh?"

The navigator grinned. "Same as for lifeboats. Every
man for himself."

The cartoon devil was back on my shoulder, telling
me that Mitchell was probably back home with Kathleen by now, doing those things in their bedroom I
wasn't supposed to think about.

Think about it, the devil said. My angel must have
come down seasick and left for the day, because I
thought about it.

CHAPTER EIGHT

The weather can change swiftly when you're at sea, especially when your ship and a drifting stormfront are moving toward one another like high schoolers playing Chicken on a back country road. By the time all the passengers were assembled on the deck for the First Mate's lecture on safety precautions, a canopy of ominous gray clouds stretched across the sky overhead.

Even though there was nothing but sea around us, I could smell the subtle promise of rain lingering in the briny air. Some people sense approaching storms in creaking joints and poorly-healed bones. I smell it. Something I picked up during my years on the golf circuit. Maybe if the real estate situation in California didn't get back on its feet the way I was hoping it would, I could hire myself out to the nightly news on some L.A. station, have them set me up in some nice top-floor penthouse where all I'd have to do was step out on the terrace and take a deep whiff, then call in the weatherman before he went on the air. They'd call me a nosecaster, right?

There were almost six hundred passengers aboard, and, as dear Mandy had forewarned us, there were no other children in sight. As we stood together listening to the First Mate, it seemed like most of the others were paying more attention to my kids than to the lecture. Truman-Paul looked back happily at them, pleased with the attention, but both Tilde and Trung seemed uncomfortable. Tilde kept glancing down at her feet, but Trung sneered a lot, as if to warn everyone that if they were expecting trouble from him, he'd be more than glad to supply it for them. I couldn't blame him.

We were all wearing life-jackets, bright orange vests that made us look like pumpkins auditioning for a Fruit-of-the-Loom commercial. The First Mate looked sure to get the part. He was a short, squat man with dark features under the brim of his cap. He addressed the English-speaking amongst us while interpreters relayed his comments to those of different lingual persuasion. ". . . and most of all, remember not to inflate your life-vests until you've reached the outside deck. If you inflate the vests inside, not more than one of you at a time can get through the door."

As he droned on, I looked over the others myself. There were a lot of couples of varying ages. Nearest to us were a pair of middle-aged New Yorkers, a husband and wife who sounded like they'd spent half their lives arguing with one another. She was trying to show him how to tie his vest while he tried to swat her hands away and insist he could manage quite well on his own, thank you. She reminded him how they'd lost a rowboat last vacation when he'd tied it to the dock with a granny knot that gave way and let the tide pull the boat out into the middle of the lake. He wondered what that had to do with putting on a life-vest and she went on about how if the cruiser went down he'd probably drown because his life-vest would fall off and the insurance company wouldn't let her collect any money because he wouldn't have drowned if he knew how to tie a proper knot. If it's true that the crochety live to an older age, I'm sure there'd come the day when they'd be quarreling over the right way to flush a zero-gravity toilet on a space-shuttle cruise of the Milky Way. By then it'd be their hundredth anniversary and they'd be as in love as ever. I was never able to figure out how couples like that managed it.

Once Kathleen and I had started going for spatting on a regular basis, usually over more petty things than knot-tying, the marriage nose-dived. Maybe it was because neither of us were the type who fought for kicks. Whether it was debating brands of deodorant or deciding on the right schools for the kids, if things got to the point of an argument, we both went for the throat or below the belt, depending on what kind of dirt we'd been saving up as ammunition. The divorce had taken most of the fight out of us. Our little scene at the airport was as ugly as things had been between us since I moved out four years ago. If Kathleen and Mitchell ever argued, I'd never heard about it.

There were some obvious newlyweds aboard, too. One couple, who looked to be in their early twenties, were taking pictures of each other putting on the life-vests, then getting someone else to take a shot of them together, smiling side-by-side. Pity the poor souls who were going to have to sit through a slideshow of their honeymoon . . .

Truman-Paul tugged on my jacket. He was pointing across the way, at a pair of identical twins in their fifties. The only way to tell them apart was that one wore a monocle over his right eye, while his brother's was over his left. They were both tall, with short hair slicked back, hawlike noses, and wide, up-turned moustaches that looked freshly tweaked. They looked like Barons in old Shirley Temple movie, the stuffy kind of aristocrats whose warm hearts were revealed with a few minutes to spare in the last reel. They saw Truman-Paul watching them and put on a little show for him, tying their life-vests with mirrored precision.

By my estimate, there were probably, a few dozen eligible singles, more of them male than female. As a rule, they were easy to spot; they had the most roving eyes. My attention fell on a young blonde standing a few dozen people away. She was my height, wearing her hair in a braided ponytail that fell over the shoulder of her sweatsuit. Her *tight* sweat suit. She noticed me admiring her and gave me a flirting smile before turning to answer a question from an older woman standing next to her.

"Don't you think she's a little young?" Tilde griped, staring up at me with a look of mild disgust. She'd caught me by surprise, and I couldn't think of anything to say, so I shifted my gaze back to the First Mate, who was wrapping up his lecture. It didn't take long for me to figure out why I was feeling tongue-tied. It was the way Tilde had looked at me and her choice of words.

Five years ago, it had been Kathleen making the same snide comment after hearing about my first affair, which had been a few-night's-stand with a waitress at the country club where I worked as the resident pro between tournaments. It wasn't something I was in the mood to think about.

Tilde wasn't about to let me off easily, though. On our way to the dining room an hour later, she was still worked up, walking along beside Trung and in front of me, just waiting for an excuse to bring it up again.

"They did everything alike!" Truman-Paul was saying excitedly. "Everything."

"Twins get that way, Truman," I told him.

"I thought twins were just *babies*," he went on. "I didn't know they got old."

"Everybody gets old, Truman."

"Except for certain young girls," Tilde slipped in, her voice thick with sarcasm.

"She wasn't *that* young, Tilde."

"She was practically *my age*."

"She was not your age, Tilde."

"She was too young."

"Men like 'em that way," Trung smirked.

I gave Trung a look that was meant to shut him up. I told Tilde, "All I did was look at her."

"Who?" Truman-Paul asked as we started down the winding steps leading to the dining room.

"Just some girl on the deck," I said.

"Which one?"

"The one with the pants too tight," Tilde taunted.

"Men like 'em tight," Trung snickered. When I glanced back at him, he grinned at me.

"Not that tight," Tilde snapped.

"Matter of personal taste," I countered. Nothing else seemed to be working, so I'd decided on honesty. If you can't be straight with your kids, who can you be with, right?

"It's a matter of medical fact." Tilde wasn't through with me yet. "You can get a *yeast infection* if your pants are too tight."

"Luckily we have medical supplies aboard," I grinned.

"What's a yeast infection?" Truman-Paul wanted to know.

"It's something we don't talk about on our way to dinner, Truman-Paul."

Reaching the ground floor of the ship, we started meeting up with other passengers, but Tilde went on as if we were still alone. "It's a disease that can be transmitted by intimate contact."

We were getting stares. I put on the embarrassed smile parents use when trying to be gracious in the face of their children's indiscretions. "Good evening," I beamed at a couple walking alongside us. "Pity about the rain," I said to someone else.

"It can even be transmitted by towels to young children," Tilde informed Truman-Paul.

"For God's sake, Tilde! All I did was look at her!"

"It was the *way* you looked at her."

"Can we drop it, please?" We were passing through the doorway into the dining room. It was a massive place, glittering with candlelight and gawdy chandeliers. Half of the passengers were already seated, working on before-dinner drinks. I couldn't wait for mine.

"Name, please?" The maitre d' asked, grabbing a handful of menus from the podium holding the reservation book.

"Tannen," I told him.

"Party of five?"

"Party of four."

The maitre d' double-checked his seating list and glanced back up at me. "We indicate you requested a table for five."

The kids were all looking at me. I conveniently remembered, "Oh, right. I did. Yes. Table for five."

The maitre d' smiled with satisfaction. He, after all, never made mistakes. "This way, please."

I led the children as we made our way past the other tables, looking for someone. Tilde caught up with me and asked, "Why do we have a table for five?"

I nodded to the young newlyweds, who were holding hands as they perused a wine list. "Good evening."

"Dad?" Tilde said.

"Hm?"

"Why do we have—"

"I just thought it might be nice to have an extra chair, Tilde, in case we ran into some lonely person. You know, someone taking the cruise on their own. Someone who needs company."

Tilde made a face. "We have to have someone *sit* with us?"

"*Who's* sitting with us?" Truman-Paul wanted to know.

Tilde whined, "I don't want that girl with tight pants sitting with us."

"Someone gonna sit with us?" Trung moaned.

I stopped and whirled around, motioning the troops to a halt. "Hey, hey. Ease off, okay? Take it easy. Will you take it easy, please? Just calm down here." Cardinal rule of child crowd control: repeat all orders and requests at least twice. "Calm down, all right?"

I'd drawn a few eyes our way and had to offer a few more winning grins and good evening's. The maitre d' veered his course and came to an abrupt halt. "Your table," he said with a gracious sweep of his arm, setting out menus before each of the place settings. "Your waiter will be Ugo. Bon Appetite."

Getting the kids seated was a major task. Once they'd decided which of the seats was the extra one, they battled to make sure they weren't sitting next to it.

"Leave it next to *him*," Tilde told the others. "*He's* the one who wants it."

Finally, we were all in place. The empty seat was to my right. I tried to reason with them. "Look, is there something wrong with providing a little space in our lives to help someone who might be traveling alone? Can you imagine what it'd be like to be alone on a big ship like this? Filled with nothing but strangers? Now, let's be generous here. We're big-hearted people."

Tilde and Truman-Paul fidgeted nervously in their chairs, having qualms of conscience. Trung was looking around the room. From the look in his eyes I could see he was up to something.

"How about *him?*" He suggested.

"Who?" I asked.

"Over there."

I craned my neck and glanced over my shoulder, spotting the man Trung was pointing at. He was old, seventy if he was a day, with thin white hair and pale skin hanging wearily from his face, giving him a mournful expression. His head was tilted slightly so that his eyes were on the age-splotched hands he held, fingers entwined, on the edge of the table before him.

"What about him?" I wondered suspiciously.

Trung raised an eyebrow. "He looks pretty lonely to me."

Tilde had spotted him, too, and her eyes widened with feeling. "Oh, he *does*. . . ."

"Some people like to be alone," I ventured.

Trung raised the other eyebrow and smiled, tickled with himself. "On a big ship like this? Filled with strangers?"

"Oh, Daddy," Tilde said with an edge of pain in her voice. "He looks like he's going to cry!"

"He's not going to cry," I said firmly. "He has a cold. You want to sit next to someone who has a cold? You want to spend your trip that way? Catching an old man's cold?"

Tilde answered, "Well, if someone has to sit here. . . ."

"No one *has* to sit here. . . ."

"Is that her?" Truman-Paul was looking back at the main entrance to the dining room, where the blonde I'd seen up on the deck had just walked in, unescorted. I pushed out my chair and stood up to get her attention. She had changed into a white dress made of soft material, cut straight across so that her shoulders were bare. Her hair was still in braids, but they were pigtails now, wrapped around her head like a woven crown of spun gold.

A prospector wearing a three-piece suit moved in and staked his claim on her before she made it as far as the maitre d'. A few other single men who had started toward her slowly drifted back to their perches at the bar.

I sat back down, unfazed, and picked up my menu. "Well, that's great. She's all set now, so we don't have to worry about her. See how simple it is?"

Before Tilde or Trung could give me a hard time, our waiter presented himself. He was Italian, with dark hair and olive skin, wearing a burgundy blazer and black bow tie. His accent was as thick as his moustache. "*Buon giorno*. My name is Ugo."

"Ugo," I mused. "Do you have a brother named Igor? Works for a doctor named Frankenstinni back in the old country?"

Ugo smiled thinly as he opened a bottle of champagne and poured it into all our glasses. The kids hadn't laughed, either. Ugo set the bottle aside and stepped back from the table. "I will be back to take your order in a minute."

He bowed slightly and drifted over to another table. I raised my glass. "*Skoal.*"

The kids seemed hesitant.

Tilde asked, "Should we drink it?"

"Absolutely. It's champagne. Come on, bottoms up."

Truman-Paul shook his head slightly. "We're not allowed."

"Who says?"

"Mom and Mitchell."

I looked around the room. "Are they on this cruise? I didn't see them." I hovered my glass forward. "*Skoal.*"

Tilde and Truman-Paul warily lifted theirs. Trung already had his right up next to mine.

"To new beginnings," I toasted, then moved my glass around, making sure it chinked with all the others.

Trung put his champagne away with no problem, but both Tilde and Truman-Paul winced squeamishly after their first sips.

"Hey, that's good stuff, you guys," I told them. "Look, I'll show you how it's done."

I jiggled my glass slightly, then drew off a sip and chased it around my cheeks like I was savoring it. Then my eyes widened with shock and I gasped with my mouth closed, forcing my cheeks to balloon and send a mist spraying out between my lips.

The kids laughed along with me. There's no warmer feeling I know than sharing laughter with your own kids. I held my glass out once again and repeated the toast.

"To new beginnings. . . ."

CHAPTER NINE

The excitement that had sustained me this far along wore off shortly after dinner and jet lag set in, demanding payment for an overdue bill. Fortunately, the kids were equally tired and I had no problems putting them to bed.

Overall, things were going great, and I laid back in my own room with my window slightly open so I could hear the sea. It didn't sound quite like the Pacific beating on the shore back in Malibu, but there was still that calming rhythm, that watery metronome of waves slapping against the hull that assures the subconscious that great and wonderful forces are at work around you. The thought of my children dozing on either side of me, separated only by a stretch of wall, filled me with further contentment. All that was missing was Kathleen at my side.

I fell asleep thinking about her, and didn't wake up until there was a knock on my door shortly after dawn the next day.

"Hey Dad? We're hungry." It was Trung.

And behold, on the second day we ate. And the third. Everyone will tell you that if there's one thing you won't be hard up for on a cruise ship, it's food. At sunrise they served snacks out on the deck, so you could nibble as you looked out past the bow, where morning light was blooming straight ahead on the eastern horizon. Back in your room, you could order up a more substantial breakfast. At eleven was soup call and more snacks offered back out on deck.

If you were a fast eater and walked fast enough to work up an appetite, you could get the noon serving of burgers and hot dogs in the grill. Then, of course, there was lunch in the dining room, where you could put in an order as late as one. The lounge provided tea and sandwiches at four. For the drinkers among us, hors d'oeuvres were set out on a table in the bar at around six. If dinner at eight didn't fill you up, you could still come back for an encore at the midnight buffet. Last call wasn't until sometime after two in the morning. Of course, we didn't marathon at all these stops the same day. We sampled every other one the first day and the rest the next. The third day we recuperated, staying for the most part in my room and playing cards while we waited for our stomachs to forgive us. We'd kept to ourselves so far, restricting our social lives to nodded greetings and a few mumbled salutations. I taught the kids how to say "hello," "goodbye," "please," "bathroom" and "thank you" in three different languages so that they'd be ready to fend for themselves later.

By the third night, we were halfway across the Atlantic, bound for the Straits of Gibraltar and the azure brilliance of the Mediterranean. The kids were starting to get restless. The weather had been bleak, another reason why we'd spent so much time in our cabins, and they were anxious for some excitement. I was happy just to share their company, but when it got to the point where even my theatrics couldn't snap them out of their antsy doldrums, we dressed up and went to catch the evening entertainment at the grand ballroom.

The show had already started. We were ushered to a

booth with a clear view of the stage, where a ventriloquist was doing a routine with a dummy that looked like a Hummel figurine with elephantiasis. Both the ventriloquist and the dummy were arguing in German. It was an interesting concept, and the audience was eating it up. Even the kids got a laugh out of it, at first. But the routine went on and I realized there was no gimmick at work here. It was simply a German ventriloquist doing a schtick in his native tongue. I leaned over and spoke with the woman in the next booth.

"Excuse me . . . uh, are you German?"

She was in mid-laughter and motioned for me to wait while she hung onto the the ventriloquist's words and then roared at a punchline delivered by the dummy. She was on the verge of tears from laughing so hard, but managed to tell me, with a coarse accent, "German-American."

I nodded and glanced around the room. "Is everyone here German-American?"

She nodded back. "We belong to the Von Steuben Society. We chartered most of the ship."

"How nice." I pulled away and let her get back to splitting her sides. The kids were giving me the evil eye. This was some kind of crude purgatory for them. Truman-Paul yawned. Thinking I might have missed it, he did it again.

"Hold your horses," I whispered to them, pointing to the Cokes I'd ordered for them. "Finish your drinks. This is a good learning experience for you."

"I already know how to drink from a glass," Tilde said with a prissy smile.

"I want a beer," Trung complained. "Maybe I'll get the jokes then."

I shook my head and looked around the room. Nice as it was to be with the kids, I knew I was going to be in need of some adult conversation before the cruise was over. The last thing I wanted to happen was for us to start getting tired of being around one another.

The blonde with braids was sitting by herself a few tables over, as perplexed as I was about the stage show. She was turned away from me, though, and I didn't want to make a play for her attention for fear of invoking The Wrath of Tilde.

I looked the other way and spotted a woman my age sitting with a group of older men. She had light, wavy hair and deep, sparkling eyes. She was laughing lightly at the show with a light, delicate chuckle that sounded like music. As she reached over for her drink, she caught me looking at her. I smiled. She smiled as she raised her glass and slowly sipped at her champagne, keeping her eyes on me.

They're all around me, I thought to myself, trying my best not to show interest. Tilde was too busy fiddling with her napkin to notice me anyway. I finished my drink and glanced back at the blonde. Now she was watching me, too. Her eyes were green, like traffic lights telling me it was okay to proceed. The ventriloquist stood up and took a bow with his dummy while the crowd applauded. I looked at my watch.

"Time for bed," I told the kids.

A rebellion was abrew. They said they weren't tired and wanted to do something else. I held my ground and managed to get them back to their cabins. By the time I'd slipped back into my cabin and started putting on a clean shirt, though, my door opened and they congregated around the room. They had their pajamas on, so I thought maybe I'd be able to send them off with good-night kisses and no hassles. I should have known better. It was time for a little three-on-one. Tilde started in first.

"I just don't understand why you're going out and we—"

I interrupted, "Because I'm a grown-up, that's why. Grown-ups go out at night."

Truman-Paul threw his arms out, exasperated. "There's nowhere to *go*!"

"You're going to look for that girl," Tilde accused.

Trung begged, "Let me go with you."

Count to ten, J.P., I told myself as I retreated to the bathroom and buttoned up my shirt. "Sorry," I said as sympathetically as I could. "Time for bed."

"We're in the middle of the ocean!" Truman-Paul exclaimed as if it were a deciding factor.

"Why can't I go with you?" Trung wondered.

I stroked my chin as I looked at myself in the mirror. No need to shave again. I told Trung, "Because I'm going to the bar."

Tilde wrinkled her nose. "Of *course* he's going to the *bar*."

"Why can't *I* go to the bar?" Trung demanded.

"Why can't you stay *here*?" I asked him.

"Why can't *you*?" Truman-Paul interrogated.

Trung stuck out his chest and bragged, "They'll serve me at the bar."

"You're too *young* to be served at the bar, Trung."

"Let him go, let him go," Tilde said with mock resignation. "Let him get a yeast infection. . . ."

"I don't want him to go," Truman-Paul whined. "I want him to stay here!"

"All right, hold it!" I raised my voice loud enough to shock them into silence, then splashed on cologne as I calmly explained, "Your father, James Paul Tannen the Third, is about to go upstairs, answering to no one, to do whatever it is grownups do, with whoever he pleases, risking whatever diseases he might find, because it's his vacation, too. "Okay?"

I grabbed a sport coat from my closet and stuffed my arms into it, then adjusted my shirt cuffs. I stared down at each one of the kids, daring them to give me any more trouble. Tilde pouted. Trung looked down at the electronic game he'd smuggled aboard the ship. That left it to Truman-Paul.

"What if I get scared?" he asked demurely.

"You'll be asleep Truman-Paul."

"I'm not tired."

"Then read a book." I'd struck a nerve. Truman-Paul cringed and looked helplessly over at Tilde. I frowned at him. "How about it, Truman. You have a hundred pounds of books packed in your room. Come on, we'll go pick one out and you can read until you—"

"No!" He bounded from bed and rushed to the door. He stood there holding it open for me. "It's okay. You can go. It's okay."

Something wasn't right, but I didn't know what.

"Truman, what is it?"

He was trembling. Stammering, he spoke with his head down. "Nothing. Just go, just go on. It's okay."

It wasn't okay. He was ready to cry. Before I could react, he rushed out and closed the door behind him. I looked over at Tilde. She turned away.

"Something about the books, is that it?" I guessed. Then I thought I had it figured out and grinned. "Dirty magazines. He's got a trunk full of dirty magazines and doesn't want me to—"

"He can't read," Trung said without looking up from his game.

"What?" I couldn't believe it.

Tilde had been sitting on my dresser, but she jumped down and pointed angrily at Trung. "You're not supposed to tell!"

I held up my hands. "Wait a second. . . ."

Still looking at Trung, Tilde said, "We promised him we wouldn't say anything."

Trung lowered his game and returned Tilde's glare. "I didn't promise him anything."

"You just like to make him look stupid!" Tilde was seething.

I stepped between them. "What's going on here?" I demanded.

Tilde bit her lips shut, but it was too late for

that. She murmured, "Truman-Paul has a learning disability."

"A what?" Not my son, I thought. No, there's a mistake here.

"Like I said," Trung repeated. "He can't read."

"Then what's in the big bag of his?" I wanted to know.

"Blocks," Tilde said. "With phonetics on them. Some with just letters." I let out a long breath, letting it sink in. Tilde looked like she was about to cry. "He was held back in the third grade last year, and if he doesn't make some progress this summer he'll have to go to a special school."

I was still stunned. "Why wasn't I told about this?"

"It's very humiliating for him. He didn't want you to know."

I left Tilde and Trung in my room and stepped out into the hallway. I was feeling a dozen different emotions all at once. What kind of a jerk-off excuse for a father was I that I didn't know my own son couldn't read? Where the hell did Mitchell and Kathleen come off not telling me about it? Where had I failed? Kathleen was a lot smarter than I'd ever be, so did that mean I was passing along learning disabilities to my kids, for Christ's sake? What else was being held back from me? Goddamnit, what was going on here?

I waited until I had myself back under control, then I knocked on the door next to mine. It wasn't locked, so I let myself in when no one answered. The lights were out and Truman-Paul was laying face-down on his bed, his face buried in his pillow.

"Tru," I said gently, coming up and sitting on the edge of the bed beside him.

"Go away," he cried, his voice muffled.

"I made them tell me."

"Go away."

I put my hand on his shoulder, trying to think of the

right thing to say, the right thing to do. He burrowed further into the bed. I got up from the bed and sat in the chair next to it. I thought a while longer. There had to be something I could do. All I could think of were grade school pep talks I used to get from my dad when I didn't want to try out for Little League because I was sure I wouldn't make the team. He'd managed to talk me into trying out. I'd sat on the bench all season, but at least I'd been able to wear a uniform and warm up the pitcher. My coach had actually proven himself to be an inspiration with his constant complaining that I swung a bat like I was trying to play golf. Thus was a star born.

"Hey, Truman," I said, just loud enough so he could hear me. "Do you know who Albert Einstein was? Smartest man in the world. And you know what? When he was a kid everyone thought he was retarded. And Sophia Loren, they thought she would be an ugly duckling all her life." I didn't get any response out of Truman-Paul, but I could hear he wasn't crying any-more. "Tru, there's a great actor, too. I forget his name, but he's got a speaking voice that would make Abraham Lincoln green with envy. When he was a kid, he used to stutter so bad he'd never talk unless he had to."

I waited. Truman-Paul turned slightly in bed. His eyes were red and his cheeks were streaked with tears. "I'll never read. I can't do it."

I stood up and leaned over him, stroking his hair. "You're going to learn how to read, Truman-Paul, be-cause I'm going to help you. I promise, okay?"

He glanced up at me doubtfully.

"Now get some sleep, son. "Don't worry." I kissed him on the forehead and eased him back into bed. He smiled feebly and closed his eyes. I went back to the door and quietly opened it. When I looked back, he was staring at the ceiling. He wasn't crying, but he had a look of sadness that tore at my heart.

"Goodnight, Truman."

"Goodnight, Dad."

"We'll lick this, you and me."

"See you in the morning," he said, then turned over on his side.

I let myself out of the room. I was ready for a drink.

CHAPTER TEN

The ship's discoteque was alive with activity and seemed worlds removed from the drama I'd just been through with Truman-Paul. Strobe lights flashed and mirror-studded globes slowly orbited near the ceiling, reflecting the glare of spotlights. A first-rate sound system punched out last year's top dance hits. And everywhere there were bodies. Bouncing and twisting on the dance floor, lined elbow-to-elbow at the bar, crammed around tables set along the walls. I might as well have been hitting a singles bar in the Marina, except that a lot of the talk around me was couched in a foreign language. I wasn't in the mood for it, but I forced myself to the bar and ordered up a double bourbon. That would snap me out of my funk if anything would.

I was starting to become familiar with some of the faces on board. I saw the monocled twins out near the edge of the dance floor, going through identical stiff-limbed moves like figures on those gimmick clocks you see in antique stores. They were straight-faced as they went through their motions, but their dance partners were in hysterics, as were a lot of onlookers. The photo-happy newlyweds were there, with the wife taking a picture of her husband mugging alongside the twins as if he were Frankie Valli and the twins were two of the Seasons. Fall and Winter, no doubt. Far off in the corner, the old man who had almost ended up joining us at our table the first night was sitting by himself, taking everything in with a lost, forlorn look as his fingers nervously tapped at the sides of his champagne glass. Maybe he'd punched up some Glenn Miller on the jukebox and was wondering when it was going to be played.

And there were lots of women. A true smorgasboard of beauty and high fashion. Most of them were taken, at least for the moment, but I was content just to look at them, for the time being. The kids had succeeded in placing a load of guilt on my shoulders, and I was beginning to think this trip would be an exercise in celibacy for me. The idea didn't disturb me greatly. Much as I fancy myself a womanizer, I've never been the type to go out looking specifically to add notches to my bedpost. I just happen to enjoy the company of the other sex. If it leads somewhere, well, if you can't be with the one you love. . . .

"Hi, Daddy . . ." Someone called out to me.

It wasn't one of my kids, unless Tilde had gobbled down a bottle of hormones when I wasn't looking. I turned around to place the voice, which seemed familiar. Mandy, the children's activities director, had wedged herself beside me at the bar. She was holding a tall drink filled with fruit, and she was out of uniform, filling out a low-cut dress layered with sequins. Her eyes and smile further confirmed that she was off duty. Perfume wafted about her like an aromatic cloud. I'm not familiar with brands, but this stuff I'd do testimonials for. One whiff and I was pointing to my empty glass when the bartender came by. It was time to buy a round for the devil on my shoulder.

"Put your babies to bed?"

"Yeah." I grinned. She kept looking at me while she sucked on her straw. Subtle, she was. I pretended not to notice and motioned out to the dance floor. "What do you think of the twins?"

The song on the jukebox had just ended and they were bowing together to their dates. "Amazing, aren't they?" Mandy said, watching them. "They're vaudevillians. Hungarian, I think. They claim they're two of identical sextuplets, but I think they're kidding."

"Imagine six of them."

"Make a great basketball team."

So much for small talk. Mandy pulled the straw out of her drink, then took a sip and gently wiped a dab of foam from her lips with her pinky. She twirled the drink's cherry between her fingers by its stem, then nibbled it.

"Divorced?" she asked.

"Uh huh."

"Gemini?"

"Very good." I was impressed. "Most people take me for a Libra."

"I looked at your passport," she confessed. When the bartender arrived with my drink, she tried again. "Scotch?"

"Bourbon. Sorry."

Mandy shrugged her shoulders, then handed her empty glass to the bartender, nodding for another round. I was already starting to feel my first drink. I was relaxed, falling into the swing of things. Mandy was studying me.

"Lawyer," she said finally.

I shook my head. "Real estate."

"I'm slipping."

I sipped some bourbon for the devil. "They just don't put enough information on passports, that's all."

She laughed. Not a timid, through-the-nose laugh. She didn't seem like the type to hold back at anything.

"How long you been doing this?" I asked her.

"Making bad guesses?" she said with a wink.

"Working on ships."

The bartender dropped off her drink and she drained off a long sample of it, enough for devils on both shoulders. She took a cigarette from her purse. I lit it and she blew smoke. If guys can imitate Bogart, it seems only fair for women to blow smoke like Bacall, if they feel like it. I don't find it all that attractive, though. I would have rather smelled the perfume and cherries on her breath.

"How long have I been working on ships?" she said. I think she was supposed to be sounding more sultry with a cigarette in her mouth, but it seemed more like her voice was hardening, like a blunt instrument she was about to use on me. "Long enough to know that if I don't play musical chairs the first few nights I won't get who I want for the cruise." She must have seen me recoiling slightly behind a false smile. "Wrong answer? This is my twelfth year. I'm hooked to it in ways. It's kind of like a luxury prison, this place. Days are regimented, meals are good, clothes are laundered, drinks are free, sex is easy, you can't get mugged or run down by a car, and all relationships end, just like they should—while hearts are still pounding and bodies are still hot, three weeks after they begin."

It was quite a mouthful and had the ring of a speech to it. I wondered how many times she'd given it. I busied myself with my drink, not sure how to handle her. I guess maybe I'm old-fashioned, but my tastes usually favor the thrill of the hunt over having the fox jump right in my lap.

She was twirling her cherry again. Even Ingmar Bergman used a little more restraint with his symbols.

"Interested?" she offered. "You have to tell me quick. Time's passing."

I laughed nervously, blinking away the smoke she'd blown lightly in my face as if it were supposed to turn me on. "Truth is, Mandy, I'm not so good under pressure."

She got over her heartbreak quick enough. Polishing

off her drink, she moved away from me, rolling her shoulders and shaking the hair from her eyes. "Fair enough," she said with a smile. "Gotta run."

She turned and was immediately asked to dance by a man who looked liked he belonged in *Gentleman's Quarterly*. They went out to the dance floor and Mandy started gyrating for all she was worth, making sure I knew what I was missing. I finished my bourbon and switched over to brandy.

I'm of the opinion that, as a rule, philosophy and alcohol don't mix. It probably comes from hearing so many drunks tumble upon would-be revelations and profundities that have about as much ring of truth as a politician's press agent. But here I was, lubricating my gearbox so I could mull over matters of great personal import. I mean, I would be turning forty by the time this cruise ended, so there seemed almost an obligation on my part to struggle with the question of *Who I Was*. The nominees weren't shaping up to be too attractive.

There was James "The Jerk" Tannen, runaway husband and father, the self-indulgent shit who lived by the dictum "What's in it for me?" and wanted nothing to do with anything or anyone that even threatened to cramp his precious style.

And J.P. "Fool" Tannen, grand schemer and dreamer of great things that could never be.

And, lastly, "Jamie the Schmoe, all blow and no show, filled with good intentions but lacking the basic backbone to follow through on anything, a man of empty promises. Well, panelists, now that you've placed your ballots . . . will the real James Paul Tannen please stand up? A tension-filled pause. Who would it be?

I got up from my stool and strode quickly through the crowd to where the blonde with braids had just sat down at a booth next to a window overlooking the deck. I gestured to the seat next to her and she smiled. I sat down, holding my snifter up triumphantly.

"Not a drop spilled." I extended my free hand towards her and introduced myself. "James Tannen." James the Jerk. The real me.

She spoke in an accent that was decidedly Scandinavian. I could only make out the last few words.

"Oh, yeah," I laughed. "Aunt Sophie? Well, I must say, you're looking in better health than at the reunion—"

"Ann-Sofie," she repeated, more slowly this time.

"Swedish?" I guessed.

Her smile widened. "Ya, Svenska."

"Swedish, eh? How about that? I speak a little Swedish, you know."

"Ya?"

"Ah yes, I haff a house un de back country. Jess a small place wiff cows un chickens un little piggies, but I don't like it so good. No sky to see from all de clouds." I was having trouble keeping a straight face. Boy was I funny. "Un de mornings I go out to be milking the cows; no sun. Night come and I look out my vindow; no moon. Very depressing. Vone day I think I have enough, so I get my gun. Vot do I do but I shoot off my toe. It hurt me like. . . ."

I was glancing up to catch her expression, which was something between confusion and annoyance, when I saw Trung, Tilde and Truman-Paul watching me from outside the bar. They'd changed into their clothes and were standing on the deck.

"I don't speak your English no good," Ann-Sofie was telling me.

"Excuse me," I told her, standing up and motioning for her to stay put. "Don't go away. I'll come back with a translator if I have to. The night is young."

She furrowed her brow, confused. When she started to turn around to look out the window, I leaned forward and held her in place by the shoulders, then raised a finger. "A minute. I'll only be a minute. Uno momento? Okay?"

I left her and hurried outside, confronting the kids. I was pissed. "What the hell are you doing up here?"

They shrank back slightly at the assault, then Truman-Paul squeaked, "The ship's leaking. There's water on my floor."

"There *is*, Dad." Tilde said with concern.

"It's in the bathroom. From the shower," Trung said, trying to get on my side. He had his eyes on the action in the bar.

"Uh-uh," Truman-Paul said, shaking his head. "It's—"

"I don't care. Get your butts downstairs, right now. Got that?" I looked at them angrily, one by one. "Am I going to have to go through this every night? Is this what's going to happen to me?"

They looked down at their feet. I'd never spanked my kids before, but I was in the mood to take them over my knee right then and there. Then Truman-Paul raised his head, breaking out his secret weapon, those large puppy-at-the-dog-pound eyes.

"I didn't memorize the number of my life-boat," he said innocently.

I sighed, turning my face so they wouldn't get intoxicated from my breath. "Just go to bed, Truman-Paul. . . ."

Tilde said, "We thought you'd at *least* come down and *check* it."

"Look, gang, I'm busy here. Do you understand that? Busy." I looked back inside the bar. My seat had just been taken by Sweden's answer to Robert Redford, some grinning schmuck with his shirt opened to his navel so he could show off the gold hanging from his neck. Is that what I'd looked like to my kids? Jesus. . . .

"When are you coming down?" Tilde asked.

Ann-Sofie was already knee-deep in conversation with my replacement.

"Now," I said wearily. "Okay? I'm coming down right now. I'll plug up the hole and save everybody on the ship. Maybe I'll get a medal and get my picture in the *Cruise News*."

We headed back toward the elevators. I looked past the railing, where the moon had poked through the clearing sky and laid a band of wavering light on the ocean. Ocean, ocean everywhere, not a trace of land in sight. I felt trapped. I was on a floating penal colony and there was no escape.

CHAPTER ELEVEN

When the electronic beeping of my travel clock yanked me out of some dream that had something to do with Heidi in a miniskirt, I knew I was in for a long, rough day. I'm the kind of guy who likes to wake up when his body tells him he's had enough sleep. Late to bed and late to rise and to hell with healthy, wealthy and wise, that's the way I see it. But I thought it was better to be woken up by an alarm than the sound of three chattering magpies spouting off ideas about the way they want to spend the day. At least you can turn an alarm off.

I wasn't as hungover as I thought I'd be, but I was feeling far from rested. It took a surge of willpower to get me into a change of clothes and out of the cabin for early breakfast. Outside, it was a gorgeous day, the first real beauty of the trip. There was a brisk cool wind but it wasn't dragging any clouds along with it. I got a table away from the breeze and the sun felt warm on my arms.

We had apparently passed by the Azores during the night and a boat from the island had ferried out some supplies, including copies of the *International Herald*. One of the things I'd missed most about the mornings was not having the chance to stick my face in the paper between bites of breakfast. Oh, we creatures of habit and our insipid needs. I had French toast, fresh juice and a small pot of coffee to go with the news that the Dodgers were back to their winning ways. Maybe I'd been wrong about the day's prospects after all.

"Morning, Dad," Trung mumbled as he slid into the seat next to me, carrying a box of Fruit Loops and a half-pint of milk.

" 'lo," I said, turning to the comics. Maybe if I ignored him he'd let me finish the paper in peace.

"They got soccer scores in there, Dad?"

"I'll give it to you when I'm finished, Trung."

"I just want to know if the Aztecs won."

"Yep," I said, although I didn't have the faintest idea.

"What was the score?"

"Four to one. Look, Trung, I'm trying to read the funnies, okay?"

"Yeah, sure, Dad. No problem." Trung's box of cereal was one of those kinds you can open from the front as well as the top. He set it down flat on the table and then started poking along the dotted lines with the handle of his spoon, humming to himself all the while. Once he had unearthed the Fruit Loops, he peeled back the foil and poured in milk so he could eat them right out of the box. They weren't Rice Krispies, so I had to wait until he'd shoveled a spoonful into his mouth and started chewing before I could hear any snaps, crackles and pops. I wasn't sure which was the more irritating, his chewing or his humming. I tried not to think about either.

"You know what I'd like, Dad?" He was talking with his mouth full. Cherry loops, orange loops, lemon loops. He looked like he was eating a rainbow. "It'd be great if you could play the video games for money instead of the slot machines. I could clean up here."

"Trung, mind your manners, would you? Who taught you how to eat?"

Trung grinned. "They don't have chopsticks here."

"Don't talk with food in your mouth."

He was already finished with the Fruit Loops. He tilted the box and drank the milk and leftover crumbs, then turned the coffee cup in front of him upright. "There enough coffee for me, Dad?"

"No, Trung, there isn't. You shouldn't be drinking it anyway."

"How come? There's no age limit, is there?"

Tilde and Truman-Paul showed up next, toting plates heaped high with croissants and breakfast rolls.

"Hey, Dad, is the water in the swimming pool from the ocean?" Truman-Paul wondered.

"I'd like to learn how to play shuffleboard today," Tilde said.

"Do they pump it into the pool or does it come from rain or what? Dad?"

"Shuffleboard's kind of like bowling, isn't it, Dad?"

"If they pump water up from the sea, how do they make sure they don't suck up a shark or something?"

Trung started complaining, "I can't go to the bar, I can't drink coffee. What a drag. . . ."

Pretty soon all three of them were talking at once. My head was starting to feel like one of those old aspirin commercials where they show lightning, knots tightening and someone beating on an anvil with a sledge hammer.

"Excuse me," I shouted. Apparently they needed a reminder that I was still upset with them over last night. They quieted down and all I heard out of them was the random bleeping of the portable video game Trung had brought with him to the table. "Do you guys ever talk to each *other*? 'Dad? Dad? Dad?' Talk to each other a little, okay? I haven't finished my coffee yet. I just like it to be . . . *quiet* . . . until I've finished the paper and my coffee. That's the way I am in the morning. Okay?"

I didn't look around for their response. I raised the paper back up to block them from view. I heard Tilde and Truman-Paul buttering their rolls, then a series of muffled electronic explosions from Trung's video game, which he'd started playing. I turned down the top corner of the paper and calmly told him, "Please don't play with that or I'll throw it off the ship." Trung glumly turned the game off and set it aside. "Thank you."

I was reading about the latest yo-yoing of interest rates in the business section when Truman-Paul cleared his throat and asked, "Dad?" When I didn't answer right off, he forged on. "What are we gonna do after breakfast?"

I lowered the paper. "We are going to find a little *space*. That's what I do *after* I've had my coffee. Find *space*." I folded the paper and set it down on the table and picked up my coffee cup, swallowing the last few sips before standing up and announcing, "Now that I've finished my coffee, I'm going to go find some space. As long as you don't high dive off the ship or tag along saying 'Dad, Dad, Dad' wherever I go, you can do whatever your little hearts desire." With a cheerful wave, I left them to each other.

There was plenty of space on the officer's deck. I had the whole area to myself and the quiet did me wonders. Back at my place in Malibu, I'd had a lot of practice staring out to sea for minutes on end, letting my thoughts run free like the dogs that raced along the beach and played tag with the tide. I thought a little about everything and everybody, trying to make sense of my place in it all—those typical cosmic musings people like to make fun of when they talk about Californians. There was no one there to bother me with their opinions, though, and while I didn't come up with any answers, I felt a hell of a lot better for it. And the time raced by. Soon the sun was directly overhead. Noon and the kids hadn't shown up yet. I almost missed them. Almost.

They weren't in the cabins when I dropped by to put on my sweat suit, but I spotted Tilde and Truman-Paul out on the lido deck when I came up to do a little working out. They were on the other side of the pool, trying to figure out how to play shuffleboard. Their sticks dwarfed them and it was easy to see they had different ideas about the rules. Trung was nowhere in sight. The area was crowded and the kids didn't spot me, so I quickly slipped up the steps leading to the extended balcony overlooking the pool. There were exercise bikes there and I figured I'd have to pedal a good dozen miles if I hoped to get rid of the paunch that had already begun to grace my waistline from the food I'd put down the past few days.

The fair-haired woman I'd seen during the ventriloquist's act the previous night was using the cycle next to mine. She was wearing a sweatsuit that revealed her to be a lusciously proportioned woman, not like the anorectic twigs that are so vogue in Hollywood and fashion magazines. Here was a woman you sensed could hold her own in any situation, not to mention any position. And she was my age, too. Who knows, maybe even Tilde might have approved. After all, she was wearing loose-fitting sweatpants.

I smiled but didn't try to interrupt her. I adjusted the tension on my bike and worked my speed up to fifteen miles an hour. A couple miles later, I had fallen into a comfortable rhythm and she had finished pedaling. She leaned over her handlebars, sucking in air greedily as she wiped a few strands of hair from her face.

Remembering that she had been laughing at the ventriloquist's routine last night, I said, "*Guten morgen.*"

She caught her breath and sat upright, returning my smile. "*Guten morgen.*"

"*Sprecken* . . . English?" I asked.

She paused a moment, then nodded.

I looked up at the bright sun and squinted. "It . . . is . . . a . . . nice . . . day."

She gave me another sample of her chimelike laughter. "Wonderful day," she said breathlessly.

I was surprised. "You *do* speak English."

"Yes." She had an accent, but I couldn't place it.

"You're not German?"

"Not German."

"I thought you were. German."

"No."

I was really wowing her with my eloquence. What other cliches could I haul out until my tongue came untied? "Where you from?"

"I live in New York," she told me.

"You have an accent."

"I was born in France."

Still pedaling, I nodded knowingly. "French."

"*Tres bien.*"

"*Tres bien.*"

She laughed again. " 'Very good'. I say 'born in France,' you say 'French.' Very smart. Very good."

She'd lost me, but I pretended I was following.

"I'm just teasing you," she said lightly, getting off the cycle. "I do that with people I like."

She said it with a genuine friendliness. None of this Mandy School of Aggressive Hustling shit. I still couldn't figure her out, but I sure wanted to try. I was pedaling faster by the second. She stepped over to a nearby weight bench and picked up the towel laying across it, then started dabbing at the glisten of sweat on her face. "I saw you in the dining room last night with your children," she told me. "Toasting champagne? I like the way you are with them. And leaving the disco last night to put them to bed? I like that a lot. It's so nice to see a man who really cares for his children. You really seem to enjoy them."

Twenty miles an hour and rising. Between breaths I bragged, "Yeah, we really have . . . fun."

"That's nice." She meant it. She seemed so sincere I was almost suspicious. Nobody's like that anymore, are they? She pulled off her sweatshirt, revealing a purple set of tights. Now I knew why they called them tights. What a woman this was. She was the kind that could keep a man from thinking about the other women in his life. I'd been looking for her type a long time. There'd been maybe two or three since the divorce.

Twenty-three miles an hour was the best I could manage and still be able to talk. "Yeah . . . we really hit it off . . . my kids and me. . . . They're great to be with."

"I can see that." She straddled a rowing machine and fit her feet into the toeholds before securing a grip on the oars. "Are you alone with them?"

"My kids? Yeah."

"There was an extra chair at your table."

"Oh, that. . . ." I slowed down. Two miles would be good enough for starters. Didn't want to wear myself out. "Uh, they made a mistake. I'm alone."

"Divorced?"

"Yeah?"

"It's great that you take such an interest in them. I hope they appreciate how lucky they are."

Ha, I thought to myself. I didn't say anything. I had two-tenths of a mile to go. I watched her row, admiring her strong arms, strong shoulders. Strong chest. She was looking to one side, and suddenly she burst into laughter. "I feel like I'm rowing the ship. It's funny." She looked up at me. "Really. Come, try it."

"Sure, why not?" I got off the bike and came over to the rowing machine next to her. She was right. We were facing the rear of the ship, and to our side we could see the ocean passing by with each stroke of the oars.

"It really feels like it, yes?"

I nodded happily. "Isn't there supposed to be some guy whipping us, though?" We both started laughing. "You know that joke? The good-news-bad-news?"

"No," she chuckled.

I shouted out like a slave-driver, "The good news is you rowers are getting steak for breakfast! The bad news is, after breakfast, the captain wants to go waterskiing!"

She laughed again, but I didn't think she understood. I rowed as hard as I could. "You know. Waterskiing. Fast."

She laughed louder and had to stop rowing. Shaking her head, she looked over at me and asked, "What is waterskiing?"

"Oh. It's kind of like snow skiing, except you're—"

"I'm teasing," she said. Standing up, she toweled herself off again. She seemed to be enjoying herself. I hoped she could tell I was, too. It had been a long time since I'd fallen in with a woman who kept me on my toes.

"I know why I thought you were German," I said, suddenly remembering.

"Yes?"

"You laughed at that dummy last night. The ventriloquist?"

"It was *funny*," she explained. "Not to understand it was *very funny*."

"Yeah," I said brightly. "That's what I was thinking at first."

"I never heard a wooden man speak German before." She laughed again and mimicked the dummy. She was incredible. If she didn't look so damn healthy I would have thought she was on drugs.

"Are you here with somebody?" I asked her, getting up from the rowing machine and trying my luck with the barbell.

"The Metropolitan Museum," she explained. "Their classical tour. I love art. This seemed like a fun way to see some."

"Is it?"

She rolled her eyes. "I'm traveling with mummies." We both laughed. So far so good. "Have you seen them? I'm serious. I'm not at all sure they're breathing."

"You'll have to have dinner with *us* sometime."

"They'd be very disappointed. At least four of them want to marry me."

I groaned slightly under the weights. "Are you in the market?" I asked nonchalantly.

She put her sweatshirt back on, then shook her hair, to get it free of her collar. "Not really. Too busy, I'm afraid. I hardly have time for a night out. To think of a husband. . . ." She made a face as she stuffed her towel into her workout bag and zipped it closed. "Not all of us divorced women are lucky to have devoted ex-husbands like you. My girls see their father . . . maybe a weekend once in awhile when he comes through town . . . a phone call on their birthdays. I'm sure you know the type."

I didn't answer her. I was too busy raising the weights over my head. God, was I out of shape! I lowered the barbell and slapped my palms clean.

"Anyway, seeing you and your children restores my faith," she said, extending a hand my way. "I'm Marie."

I took her hand greedily. "J.P. Tannen."

"J.P."

"James."

"Hello."

"Hello."

She took her hand back. "Good-bye."

Oh well, I thought. "Good-bye."

It was a bizarre exchange, and we both snickered at the way it sounded. Think of something else to say, Tannen!

"*Au revoir*," she said, taking a step back.

"*Au revoir*."

"Very good!"

"*Tres bien?*" I smiled slyly.

"Excellent!" She turned around and started up the steps leading to the upper deck. I watched her, wondering if we'd end up getting together again. There was something about her that made me want to take her apart and see what made her tick. On the other hand, I also wanted her to remain mysterious and filled with elements of the unknown. It was so refreshing to meet a woman of substance.

I was still watching her when I heard whispered voices carried in the breeze. I couldn't place them, but I knew it was Tilde and Truman-Paul. Wherever they were, it wasn't the shuffleboard court.

"He's still looking at her," Truman was saying.

"Men always watch women when they go away."

"How come?"

"Their butt," Tilde was explaining. I looked around but still couldn't see them.

"Their butt?"

"I hope you don't get that way, Truman-Paul."

"Are you kidding: Why would I want to look at a butt?"

I finally spotted them, hiding behind the upstairs railing, spying on me. I wasn't angry at them, though. I had a new reputation to live up to.

CHAPTER TWELVE

There was an afternoon film showing in the ship's
theatre at two and both Tilde and Truman-Paul wanted
to go. Trung was on the loose somewhere, and he's not
a big fan of anything on a screen that's not connected to
a game cartridge or joystick, so we left a message in the
cabin telling him where we were and went to the movies. It was a foreign action film dealing with pirate
adventure on the high seas. The showing before had
been in German and the evening show was dubbed in
Swedish, so we'd picked the right time to go. It was a
dumb movie, but we had a great time anyway, filling
up on junk food and sitting up front together.

Truman-Paul always used to drive me crazy at
movies because he couldn't keep quiet for more than
five minutes at a stretch, but this afternoon he was on
his best behavior, speaking out only to join Tilde and me
in cheering with the audience for the good guys to put
down the climactic assault by pirates wearing cheap
wigs and T-shirts over jeans cut short at the shins. It
was one of those films that are so bad you can't help but
root for them, provided you didn't have to pay admission.

Afterwards, I left Tilde off with a group of elderly
women playing shuffleboard on the recreation deck.

She immediately became the cruise's surrogate grand-daughter, and I had trouble getting away from them with Truman-Paul in tow. He and I had some things to work on.

He had become apprehensive as soon as I had indicated that we were dropping Tilde off, and when I told him we were going to his cabin, he seemed as if he were about to become visibly ill.

"Come on, Truman," I cajoled him as we came into his room and I closed the door on us. "That's no kind of attitude to have."

"I don't want to do it." He was getting stubborn now.

"Well, you've got a long life ahead of you, Tru, and there's going to be a lot of things you won't want to do, but you're going to have to do them anyway. Now's as good a time to start getting used to it as any." I reached for the blue bag resting on his dresser and shook the blocks out onto the bed.

"I can't," Truman-Paul said, staring at the blocks fearfully, as he stood up against the wall farthest from the bed.

"Of course you can, Truman," I assured him patiently. "It's simple."

"Not for *me!*"

I separated a few of the letter blocks and set them out randomly on the bedspread in front of us. "Okay, the word we're going for is 'policeman.' Here, I'll start you out. 'P.'" I made the letter's sound a few times, then asked him, "What comes next? Come on over here and try."

He approached the letters as if they were aliens from outer space. Unfriendly aliens at that, the kind that would zap him if he got too close. I'd never seen him so alarmed.

"Just listen to the way it sounds, okay?" I mouthed the word slowly. "Pooooo . . . Pooooo . . . leeeeeeese

. . . man. Po–lice–man. Now, what letter comes after 'P'?"

He sat at the edge of the bed and concentrated on the blocks, his lips pressed tightly together. He looked up at me and said hopefully, " 'S'?"

I took a deep breath. "No, Truman. That's wrong." I pointed to the letters, trying to keep my temper in control. "There's no 'S' here, is there? We're just dealing with these letters here. Now try again."

"I *told* you I can't do it!"

I got up and started pacing the room. "I want you to stop saying 'can't,' Truman," I insisted. " 'Can't' means 'won't.' Do you understand that? There's nothing in this world you can't do if you really *want* to. The whole key is *wanting* to. Now, do you *want* to read, or don't you?"

"Yes."

"Good. Then you will."

"I *won't*."

"Try it again. Look, watch me when I say it, okay?" I pointed with my finger, rounding my lips like I was about to blow smoke rings. "Pohhhhh . . . Pohhhhh-hhhhh . . . Pohhhhhhh—leeeeeeese—man. Poh, Poh, Poh . . ."

Truman stared at my mouth, even mimicked the way I had my lips. Then he said, " 'A'?"

I threw up my hands in disgust. " 'A'? Truman, it's not 'pal–eese–,an.' It's not 'paul–eese–man.' It's 'pohhh-hhhhh–leeeese–man'. Poh!"

"I can't do it!" he wailed.

I started yelling at him. "You're going to read before this trip is over! Do you understand that, Truman? You're going to do it because you're going to put in the kind of effort that people *have* to put into things to get results. You are not just to float around the ocean these next few weeks saying 'I can't'!"

Frustration and anger boiled over into tears, and Truman took a vicious swipe at the letters, sending them flying from the bedpsread.

"I can't!" he howled defiantly, springing to his feet and bolting for the door.

"Truman!" I shouted after him, but he was already gone. I took up the chase, cursing myself for what I'd done. What the hell did I know about correcting learning disabilities anyway? What was I trying to prove by leaning on him like that? Was it him or me I was really angry with? Or was it Kathleen and Mitchell, for leaving me in the dark? All I knew for sure was that I'd screwed things up royally, the way I always did.

I saw Truman turn the corner down the far end of the hallway and picked up my stride, calling out his name again. When I rounded the corner, I almost collided with an officious-looking steward dressed in white with a graying goatee. I apologized and slowed down a little. To my surprise, he followed alongside me.

"Are you Mister Tannen?" he asked. His accent was British. We had a regular United Nations aboard here.

"Yes I am."

Staying with me as I started down the steps after Truman-Paul, the steward said, "Could I speak to you for a minute, please?"

I bounded down the steps with him still behind me. "Look, I'm in kind of a hurry right now . . ."

"It'll take just a moment, Mr. Tannen . . ."

"I really can't talk right now . . ."

"The captain asked that I speak to you about your son." That slowed me down. "The Chinese boy."

We were at the bottom of the steps. I stopped and said, "He's from the Phillipines. What about him?"

"Well, sir in the last hour or so, he's been asked to leave three different locations on the ship."

"What do you mean?"

"Well, he was asked to leave the pool for being a bother to the other passengers; he was asked to leave the galley, where no passengers are allowed and he was

seen taking sandwiches; and he was just asked to leave
the bar after ordering two piña coladas which he signed
for using a false identification that said he was twenty-
two years of age."

I'm glad there were no mirrors around, because I
don't think I would have liked seeing the look on my
face. What was I going to hear next, that Tilde was
playing the old ladies for money and bilking them out of
their Social Security checks for the next five years?

"We thought you'd want to be advised," the steward
said.

What could I say? I thanked him and went on trying
to catch up with Truman-Paul. He'd gained too much
ground on me, though, and was nowhere in sight out on
the deck. I asked other passengers and crew members if
they'd seen him, but no one had. More than a few of
them shot me rude looks that gave me the idea they
knew I was Truńg's father as well. I started looking for
him, too. I hoped I'd find him before I found Truman-
Paul. Tru had had enough of my temper for one day.

After an hour of scouring the ship, I hadn't found
either of the boys and Tilde had disappeared from the
shuffleboard courts, too. One of the old ladies told me
she was going to early lunch. The more I thought about
it, the more likely it seemed that I would find the boys
there, too. What better place to avoid discipline than in
the most crowded room on the entire ship?

Sure enough, Trung was sitting at our table, caught
up in his portable video game. I came over to him and
asked, "Where are the others? I've looked all over this
damn ship for Truman-Paul."

"He's in the boiler room," Trung said calmly, not
looking up from his game.

"What's he doing in the boiler room?"

"Sweating, probably."

"Funny boy," I said sarcastically, emphasizing 'boy.'
"Where's Tilde?"

"Talking to the old man."

"What old man?"

"The one who eats alone. His wife was supposed to come with him, but she died instead."

I looked around for them. "I don't see her."

"They're in the card room." All this time he hadn't looked up from his game for more than second or two. I just stood in front of him until he acknowledged me. "You mad?" he asked.

"I'm mad," I said as calmly as I could. It was no use. The best I could do was keep the rage nonviolent. "What the hell were you doing in the bar ordering pina coladas?"

"You'd have thought I'd accused him of murder. "Me?"

"You."

He cocked his head as if he were still surprised. "Who said that?"

"You're telling me you weren't?"

He set down his game and looked up at me blandly. "So, what's the big deal?"

"You're fourteen years old, *that's* the big deal."

"Big deal."

"Yeah, big *deal*. And what the hell are you doing, bothering people at the pool, and swiping food in the galley? What the hell's going on with you?"

He had his favorite smirk on his face, the one that tried to say he was God's gift to the universe and that anyone who couldn't see it wasn't worth the bother of enlightening. He was asking for it. "And how do you get off using an I.D. that says you're twenty-two years old?"

People were just starting to come in for dinner, and I could see them moving to other parts of the room. Ugo, our waiter from the previous nights, watched the confrontation with a disinterested air from his post near the wine racks.

Trung had no ready answer, so he picked his video game back up and punched up another game.

"Quit playing with that goddamn thing!"

He shut it off. For the first time, I saw a glimmer of fear in his eyes, hiding behind the facade of bravado.

I held my hand out towards him, open palm up. "I want it." When Trung started to hand over the game, I shook my head firmly. "The I.D."

Trung pretended he hadn't heard or understood me.

"Hand it over," I repeated.

"I don't have it!"

"One of us is going to tear it up. I want the whole thing or I want it in pieces."

"It cost me a lot of money," Trung complained.

"I want it."

A disgusted look came over his face and he looked around the room, hoping to gain some sympathy from the other passengers. I leaned over slightly, blocking his line of vision, staring him down. "You know what it took me to get you on this ship? You especially, because you're not even a citizen yet? I had to wait in line at embassies every Wednesday and Friday for the past two months! Now, if you think you're going to repay me by making my life miserable, you've got—"

Trung pushed away from the table and tried to get up. I put my hand on his shoulder and held him down. "Sit back down. I'm not finished yet."

He shoved my hand away and lunged from his seat again, spitting, "Kiss off, man . . ."

I grabbed hold off him and nearly flung him back into his chair. "Don't you *dare* talk to me that way!"

"Why not!" he fumed.

"Because I'm your father."

"Who says?"

We faced off, both seething while we waited for the next escalation. Tilde wandered into the militarized zone.

"Dad?" she said sweetly to get my attention. I looked over and saw the old man standing just behind her. "This is Mister Peachum. Can he use our extra chair today? I told him you ordered an extra chair for—"

"Tilde . . ." I cut her short and looked past her at

Mister Peachum. He was well-dressed and had a benevolent, expectant look on his face, but he was wary of looking back at me. "Tilde . . . we're having a few problems here today."

Tilde was taken aback. "But I *invited* him . . ."

The old man cocked his head to one side, straining to hear. "What's that?" he wheezed.

I raised my voice, an easy feat under the circumstances. "I said this might not be the best day."

"What?" He was squinting intently at my face and I realized he was trying to read my lips. I spoke slowly and exaggerated the words, like I'd just tried to do with Truman-Paul in his room. "To have lunch with us. Perhaps another day."

Tilde's face was turning red with embarrassment. Mister Peachum finally caught on to what I was saying and raised an eyebrow, trying not to show his disappointment. "Oh. No problem, no problem." He turned and started to hobble off. He told Tilde with a sad smile, "You just let me know."

Once Mister Peachum had retreated to his own table, Tilde turned on me, angry tears welling in her eyes.

"How *could* you . . . ?"

"I'm sorry, Tilde." I was. I was sorry about a lot of things, and only a few of them were happening just then.

Tilde was far from appeased. "You said that chair was for lonely people . . ."

"Lonely *girls*," Trung corrected cynically.

"I've had enough from you, Trung" I warned.

"He was so happy to be invited," Tilde wept.

Truman-Paul shuffled onto the scene, face down. He slipped into his chair and declared, "I'm not eating."

"Can I go to my room?" Trung asked.

"How could you do that?" Tilde sobbed. "I could die!"

"Then call him *back*!" I burst out angrily, startling her and the others. At that point, I didn't care. Half the room was looking on by now, including Marie. "Or go eat with *him*!" I raved on. "Do what you want. All three of you. You want to go to your room, Trung? Go ahead. You're not hungry, Truman-Paul? That's fine. I'm not either. Jesus Christ, I thought we were going to have a good time here. That's all I wanted. A good time, pure and simple. But I see that's not in the cards, so you guys just go ahead and do whatever the hell you want!"

"That's no way to talk to children!" Tilde said through her tears. Truman-Paul and Trung were still shocked by my outburst.

I was about ready to cry myself. I looked at the three of them sitting there, and I could feel a sense of failure piercing me as surely as a stake through the heart.

"You're right, Tilde," I confessed, struggling to keep my voice from faltering. "I don't know how to talk to children. I never did."

For the second time that day I left them at the table and made a hasty exit from the dining room. I needed more than a drink.

CHAPTER THIRTEEN

I was back in bed, where the day had begun on its sour note twelve hours before. It had been the kind of day that had driven me out of my marriage five years before. Up and down, up and down, from giddy highs to miserable lows in the blink of an eye. Life in the rollercoaster lane. I couldn't handle it. Me, I like operating on a nice, level course, preferably on some upper plateau of happiness. It was worth it to forego a ration or two of ecstacy if it meant not having to put up with bouts of the dark, hard funk and anger. Why did life have to be so god damn difficult?

I remembered what a change Kathleen and I had gone through after Tilde was born. She'd been a colic baby, a real screamer. And she didn't keep any regular schedule for her outbursts, although her favorite times for crying usually seemed to be a few minutes after I was asleep. I've already said how much I hate being woken up when I haven't had enough sleep. With Tilde it would happen at least three or four times a night. It's hard to convey how agonizing it is to be filled with so much love for a child and find yourself waking in a rage because she won't stop crying once she starts. Kathleen was able to handle the situation with few problems.

She'd always been patient to a fault, and she just adjusted herself around Tilde's needs, the way any decent parent would. I couldn't adjust. I put out feelers to have myself booked on as many golf tours as I could, claiming we'd be needing the extra money. The real need, though, was my need to get away from the let's-sacrifice-everything-for-the-baby syndrome. I got away on a cross-country tour for a six-month stretch, during which I played the best golf of my life and made enough money to stock up a nestegg we could live off for awhile. I called home at least once a day and flew back whenever I had a few days off. It was a good arrangement. For me. I really didn't give that much thought to Kathleen's or Tilde's needs. Kathleen seemed content enough to see me happy and Tilde, well, she was just a baby, although one that was growing by leaps and bounds.

When the cross-country tour ended, I landed a job as golf pro at one of the courses near home. Tilde was over the colic and I wanted time with her and her mother. I wasn't a complete jerk, after all. I wanted to have my arms around Kathleen while we watched Tilde reach her wondrous milestones. Her first "goo goo." The bronzing of her first booties. "Da-da" and "Ma-ma!" Her first time standing up, clinging her pudgy fingers around my pinky, drooling as she held on for dear life. Gooey fingers as she dismantled her first birthday cake and threw it on the new carpeting. The glint of thrill in her eyes as she took her first steps. Getting to know the counter people at the camera store on a first name basis because I was taking so many pictures of her. Granted, there were hard times when Tilde would come down with fevers and infections and blotches and we were constantly horrified that she might die until the pediatrition inevitably chuckled and told us not to worry. She tried to swallow one of my golf balls once but couldn't fit it in her mouth before we got to her (thank God I didn't play professional marbles). But all in all it had been a pleasurable magical time.

It was a time of change for both Kathleen and me, but with her it was less dramatic, more secure. Her world had become centered around motherhood and the home. It was what she wanted, and she was content with it. But I still had my golf and that whole world outside the home to deal with. It wasn't enough for me to be a husband and father. I loved my game, loved the chance to see my name and face in the sports page, loved the fringe activities that came with touring. I went back on the road for another year. I called home every other day . . . well, sometimes only twice a week. My game had slipped a little, but I still fared well enough to send back money to pay bills, come home for holidays and feed the nest egg.

Then came Truman-Paul, and I was home for another two years. He was a better baby as far as not crying went. Tilde had long since turned into a sweetheart, too, and we considered ourselves one big happy family. We moved into a larger house in a better part of town, within walking distance of the golf course. Kathleen was able to bring the children over so that we could have picnics during my lunch hour. We had access to the lake that provided the course with its water hazard, and summers we'd spend long hours on the strip of beach beyond range of stray balls, with Tilde and I building sandcastles for Truman-Paul to demolish while Kathleen watched on, knitting or crocheting something new for the kids.

Those were the times of the high plateau, when things seemed to move along at that happy, manageable level. Then it all started to slowly come apart. Looking back, there didn't seem to be any major event that triggered it. It was probably a combinations of circumstances, like it is for most things. Tilde started school, Truman-Paul started coming down with a string of bizarre ailments that kept him going back and forth between the hospital and home, eating up our savings and making him so temperamental that I wished he'd had had colic as a baby instead, he was such a trial to be around. The golf course changed ownership and the new management had somebody else in mind to be the resident pro. The lake became choked with algae and they closed down the beach while they started dredging up the bottom. I got tired of local tournaments and decided to quit my job at the course, which had been miserable ever since the new owners took over. I fell into an opportunity to go on a few international tours and went for it. It all flowed as sort of a natural progression over several years, and before I really had a chance to give it much thought, I'd drifted away from my family.

I had a few flings on the road and started getting a reputation for being somewhat of a playboy, and word naturally made its way back home, usually a few hours or days before my urgent calls to say it was all lies hyped up by the press.

Through all this Kathleen had been as understanding and supportive as she could be, and certainly more than she had any reason to be. I could come home at any time and find myself in the embrace of loving arms, and the kids would always shriek with delight, hoping this time I'd be staying longer than a few days or weeks. It didn't work out that way. If there wasn't another tour lined up, I'd somehow find another reason to get away.

Don't get me wrong. I'm not a man without a conscience. Throughout all the running away and philandering, the worm of guilt was always there, slowly eating away at me. There would be those lonely nights in hotel rooms when I'd take out my wallet and look at the pictures of my family and wonder bitterly what I was trying to prove, what point or purpose I was trying to make of my life. But those nights passed, and they were few and far between. Most nights there were parties and dinners, golf buddies and stray women looking for a good time. It was easy to distract myself. And somehow, through it all, I managed to play a decent game of golf.

It was during my tour in the Phillipines that it dawned on me that I'd neglected my marriage and my family to the point where I stood a chance of losing both. I'd come back to my hotel after finishing my qualifying round for the tournament. There was a message at the desk for me, saying that Kathleen had called, trying to get in touch with me. It was the first time she'd been the one to call, so I knew it had to be urgent.

I put through a long-distance call immediately, but there was some kind of trouble with the lines and it had taken five hours before I could get through, during which time I had anguished over the grim possibilities of what had happened back home. I was certain that the Fates had stepped in and orchestrated some tragedy to pay me back for all the sins of neglect I'd made against my family. I pleaded with those Fates to prove me wrong, promising I'd do anything if only I'd hear that everyone was fine. My call was finally put through and I got Kathleen on the other line. It turned out I hadn't called Truman-Paul on his birthday the day before and *she* was worried that something had happened to *me*. I was so relieved that it hadn't occurred to me to make up some lie about having tried to call. Half-laughing to get the anxiety out of my system, I confessed that I had completely forgotten about Truman's birthday. There was a pause on the line, then she said a few short words and hung up on me. *You son-of-a-bitch.* Into those five words she'd squeezed years of pent-up pain and frustration, and even with the phone connection as bad as it was, the cold fury of those words ripped through me more than anything I'd experienced in my life.

We humans sometimes fall prey to strange quirks of logic, and I was ripe for the picking after being devastated by Kathleen's call. It was the next day that I first met and decided to adopt Trung. I still don't fully understand how it came about. Maybe it was the fact that Kathleen's rage had left me so vulnerable that when I saw Trung I saw my own children—cast off and

hungry-eyed for attention and love, following me around
and looking to me as a savior of sorts. I don't know. I
took him in and two weeks later we were both in New
York, now father and son in hopes of putting back
together a family that had fallen apart.

I tried. We all tried. But it didn't work. We were
together for close to a year, putting up a valiant facade,
going through the motions of being a happy family. But
something had happened. I didn't fit in. Even Trung
had an easier time becoming a natural fixture in the
family than me. Of course, he didn't have a list of past
failings to overcome like I did. I tried, maybe too hard.
It finally became clear that there was too much falseness
to go on. Mitchell had already come into Kathleen's life,
so I tried to blame it on him. I used him as my excuse
to pack up one day and move to California on my own.
California, during the height of the me-decade. It was
the mecca for those seeking that constant plateau of
manageable happiness, the life without great ups and
downs. The life of the laid-back.

Christ, what a life. . . .

I was wading farther into these waters of self-pity,
working up the nerve to dive headlong into a night of
sleepless misery, when I heard a knock on the door.

"Who is it?" I glanced over at the clock. Only half-
an-hour had passed since I'd left the dining room.

Nobody answered, so I got up and opened the door.
Tilde and Truman-Paul were standing side-by-side, looking glumly up at me. I didn't know what to say, so I
just looked back at them. I felt numb and useless.

"We want to call our Mom," Truman-Paul said.

Fair enough. What else should I have expected?

"Okay," I said flatly.

Truman said, "The Captain said we needed your
permission."

"You've got it."

"Thank you," Truman-Paul said formally.

"You're welcome." We were like diplomats wrapping up a hard-fought bargaining session.

"We'll place it during dinner so you won't have to look at us when you eat."

They turned and left, joining up with Trung at the end of the hallway. Tilde hadn't said a word. I closed the door and muttered to the wretch staring at me in the mirror, "You son of-a-bitch."

CHAPTER FOURTEEN

Scheduled cocktail parties around the swimming pool had been cancelled the previous two nights due to inhospitable weather, but tonight the skies were still clear and there was only a slight breeze blowing, and that was far from uncomfortable. The party was on, and the air was festive with the celebrative mood of the passengers crowding the deck. Colored lights were strung along the balconies, spaced between curls of twisting crepe paper. A band was playing old favorites near the pool, and the sound carried far out into the night. Bartenders were kept busy at the portable bars, and kitchen help kept the snack table well-stocked with hors d'oeuvres. The dancing was far more subdued than at the disco. Partners went through their steps arm-in-arm, dancing close together. It was a night meant for romance.

I sat alone on one of the dozens of chaise lounges lining the deck above the proceedings, with a sour, tortured look on my face, like the Grinch stewing with his hatred for Christmas in my favorite Dr. Seuss book. I'd been there since sunset, having retreated from my cabin before the kids had come back from supper. I wasn't ready to face them yet. I was too busy confronting myself.

I'd done a lot of idle bragging about the extent to which I'd supposedly changed going into this cruise, but now I kept thinking back to my exchange with Kathleen at the airport. I hadn't fooled her for a second. Much as I had denied her stream of accusations about my deficiencies of character, I knew now that she had been right on all counts.

I was unreliable.

I was selfish.

I was a dreamer.

I had no real sense of commitment to anyone but James Paul Tannen. I was trying to muscle my way back into my kids's lives with this grandiose cruise to satisfy my needs, not theirs. They were already taken care of, more than I could ever hope to take care of them. What was it Kathleen had said? Something about people not changing their lives to suit my whims. And that I should respect their happiness. Leave well enough alone. I'd blown my chance with them. The least I could do was keep from mucking up their lives any more than I had. Kathleen was right. I should take them to Egypt and let Mitchell take take them to the dentist.

So where did that leave me? Free and easy. The hit-and-run father. Now you see him, now you don't. They had their lives. I owed it to myself to have mine. I was on the verge of forty. Maybe it was time for me to acknowledge my failures and move on; make a forward change instead of trying to step back and recreate a past that could just never be again. I'd lost Kathleen. There was no sense in thinking I could ever have her back. And the kids . . . well, I'd have to be content with being the kind of person they wanted me to be, even if that person wasn't a father who would be there when they needed him.

The band had stopped playing and I was able to hear the steady murmur of conversation below, accented by the chinking of glasses and an occasional burst of laughter. All that joy down there, making a mockery of my loneliness. I must have been a pathetic sight, sitting there and languishing in depression.

I had no idea I was being watched until a sudden gust of wind alerted me to the sound of fluttering cloth nearby. I turned in my seat and saw Marie standing a few yards away, a shawl wrapped around her shoulders. Her hair was pulled up and she was wearing a dark cocktail dress that seemed to have been made for her. She was looking at me with a slight, tentative smile, but I could see worry in her eyes. They say misery loves company, and just the sight of her was enough to shake me slightly from my mood. A drowning man will panic a little less if his hands brush against something he can hold onto.

"Hi," she said softly, taking a step closer. "I saw you from down there. No parties for you?"

I smiled stiffly and shook my head, then nodded slightly when she pointed to the lounge chair next to me. She sat down and we both looked out past the railing at the night sky. There was only a small wedge of moon and a scattering of stars showing.

"It's not easy being a parent, is it?" she said.

I was startled at first. Just who was this woman? Someone I conjured up in place of the devil who usually whispered to me from that side? She was looking at me knowingly, and I wondered if I'd been talking out loud to myself without realizing it.

"No, it's not," I finally managed to stammer.

More silence passed. Down below the band started a slow waltz and was awarded with a round of applause by passengers moving to the dance floor.

"With my three girls sometimes I get so . . ." She paused, seeking out the right word. " 'overwhelmed'? I get so overwhelmed I could scream. I actually have visions of running away. That's why I'm on this cruise, really. My friends talked me into it. They said I'd go crazy if I didn't get away. And yet I love them, and miss them so much. I hardly know who I am without them."

The lilt of her accent was as soothing as the play of rippling waves on a calm sea. I could have listened to her talk for hours.

"I wonder if it's the same for a man." She turned to me. "Is it?"

I didn't know what to tell her. I just sat there. She'd been talking as if she knew my thoughts anyway. Maybe I was hoping she'd read my mind and make sense of it for me.

"I don't know," I finally whispered dejectedly.

She nodded to herself and looked back out past the railing. I wanted to thank her for coming up and talking to me, but I was wary of giving her the wrong impression. I'd said so many of the wrong things lately, I was afraid if I opened my mouth I'd scare her off.

"*Alore*," she sighed.

"*Alore?*"

" 'So.' "

"So . . ."

"*Alore*," she sighed again.

I'd been so absorbed with myself, I hadn't paid that close of attention to her, to who she really was and why she was sitting here next to me. She was no figment. She was here for hersef as well as me, I realized. How big of me.

"My girls . . . get very . . . 'strange' . . . to see me with another man. They don't like it. Is it the same for you? I mean, if they see you with a woman?"

I thought of Tilde and smiled to myself. "They don't like it."

"No. I suppose . . . it's their loyalty to the other parent. I only know that they get angry. Especially if they sense I'm interested. So . . . I don't often get involved. I'm not even sure . . . I know how to go about it . . . anymore." She looked at me pensively, and the vulnerability in her eyes struck me. She was a

lot like me. One of the walking wounded. "I suppose
. . . they'd be 'angry' with me . . . right now."

She looked away, nervous and embarrassed. I felt as
if someone had snuck up behind me and stole my spine
from beneath my skin. I couldn't move, and I was still
afraid to speak for fear of spoiling the moment. It was
like being back in high school, squirming through my
first date. She was just as uncomfortable.

"I think . . . when you speak a foreign language . . .
it's difficult to be . . . 'subtle'. What I feel is . . .
'subtle.' What I feel is . . ." She let out a sigh and
started to stand up. "I feel stupid. As I said, I don't
know how to do this anymore."

I couldn't let her leave.

"You're doing great," I assured her. "Don't go away."

She almost collapsed back into the chair with relief. I
looked at her and smiled. "Listen. We're the only two
people on this ship who don't understand that ventriloquist's dummy. We've got to stick together."

She relaxed a little and laughed. I got my spine back
and sat up. "Marie, how would you like a drink?"

"I would *love* a drink."

I stood up and helped her to her feet. She held my
arm as we walked down the deck. Neither one of us was
drowning anymore.

CHAPTER FIFTEEN

We each had a quick drink on the deck, then retreated to Marie's room with a bottle of chablis. While I wrested the wine into an ice bucket, I noticed the personalized touches she'd added to the cabin. There was a poster of the New York skyline on one wall and a blown-up picture of two young ballerinas on the wall right next to me.

"Your daughters?" I asked.

She shook her head as she hung up her shawl and put it in the closet. "Take a closer look at the girl on the left."

I leaned forward. The image wasn't clear because of the enlargement, but I was still able to make out the features. "It's you! Amazing! So you're a dancer?"

"*Was.* Long ago, when I was much younger and much thinner." She came over to where I was standing and rotated the bottle in the ice, then took a corkscrew from the top of the dresser and opened it. "Excuse me, but I'm very thirsty."

"Ditto." I set wine glasses out for her to fill, still admiring the picture of her. "Did you dance professionally?"

"Oh, heavens no!" She sipped her wine and raised

103

her eyebrows, pleased with the taste. "I wasn't that good at it. It was mostly a fun thing for me. I liked the discipline and the atmosphere. I still practice when I have the the chance."

"Did you give it up when you had children?"

I'd hit a nerve. Her smile stiffened and she turned away from me.

"I'm sorry," I said. "I didn't mean to—"

"No, no, that's fine." When she looked back, her composure had returned. She nodded at the picture. "The other girl was my best friend. For many years we practiced together and always told each other that we would become successful at the same time. You know, silly promises. We knew each other's secrets and dreams and were always there for each other. Then one day she came late to practice and had a long look on her face, as if she was ashamed. Her eyes were red from crying, and when I asked her what was wrong, she started to cry again. She told me that she had gone to an audition on the other side of town, for a part she wanted very much. She hadn't told me because she was afraid if I tried out too I might have gotten the part. Now she had the part and was sick that I wouldn't forgive her for not telling me. I didn't think it was so big of a thing, at first, but the more I thought about it, the more I was hurt. It turned out that she had to go on the road to be with the show, and when she left the next week I never saw her again.

"I was engaged to be married at the time, and I remember there was one night when I was feeling very angry at my friend and at myself for what had happened, so I decided that I would get pregnant so I would have an excuse for not becoming as successful as my friend. She was famous for a time . . ." She paused to see my reaction. "This is not much of a story, is it. I don't mean to bore you."

I grinned. "*Au contraire*."

She laughed lightly and raised her glass. "I like you, James."

"To friendship, then," I toasted.

She took a final, whimsical look at the picture while resting the side of her glass against her chin. "I still think of her as a friend. Sometimes I think if I had had a chance like her, I might have done what she did, too."

"Did you ever try to get back in touch with her?"

She shook her head, crossing the room and picking up a framed photograph from the commode next to her bed. "These are my girls. Would you like to see them?"

"Very much." I came and looked. I could tell it was a recent picture, because Marie looked pretty much unchanged. She was crouched down with her daughters gathered around her. It was easy to tell them apart by age, and they all bore a faint resemblance to their mother, although one of them had dark straight hair. That one was the middle one in age, and she stood behind her mother. The youngest and oldest daughters were both confined to wheelchairs, sporting wide smiles and thick sets of braces around their thin, misshapen legs.

"Carmen, Angela, and Louise," she said proudly, pointing them out to me.

"They're lovely."

"I love them very much."

I pointed to Angela, the one standing. "Is that what your husband looks like? I mean, does she have his—"

"My ex-husband," Marie corrected me quickly. I was taken off-guard by the trace of irritation in her voice. She noticed it, too, and lightly touched my arm as she set down the photo. "Forgive me, James. I did not mean to sound angry."

"No problem."

Marie took a long sip from her glass, then walked back over to the dresser and refilled it. I watched her carefully. It was as if she were struggling to hold back something deep inside her, something that was trying hard to get out.

"Want to talk about it?" I asked.

Her face reddened slightly and she stared at the floor. "Maybe already I have said too much, James."

"Marie . . ." I said softly. She looked up at me. "I'll listen."

She leaned against the dresser, holding her glass with both hands. As she spoke, she kept looking across the room at the picture by her bed.

"Carmen was born first. It was less than a year after I was married. She had a birth defect. You can see from just looking at her. The doctors said it was something that had to do with our genes. I had a grandfather and an aunt who were born crippled. They said that there was always a chance that any other children I had would be born the same way. A small chance, but still a chance.

"My husband wanted a son. He is an Italian, very macho. He would not be happy without a son. So we had Angela, a healthy baby. Yes, she does look a lot like her Poppa. But she was not a son.

"Then we had our third child, another daughter. Louise looked just like Carmen when she was a baby. So sweet it made you cry to look at her legs. But not my husband. He was . . . fed up. He said that because I could not give him a healthy son he had no choice but to go find another woman to share his good genes with. That is when he left me. He was moved out before I came home from the hospital. . . . Later, after he had his son by a new wife, he became guilty and began to send money and birthday cards. I did not want any part of him, but my daughters were excited to know they had a father after all, and we needed the money, so. . . ." She looked at me, blinking back tears as she laughed nervously. "So, you see, I am full of stories."

"Marie. . . ."

"I think you should go," she said. "It is wrong for me to invite you to my room just to burden you with my problems. I should be ashamed of myself."

"I'm here because I want to be, Marie," I told her evenly, holding out my glass. "I think I should stay."

She wiped at her eyes with the back of her hand, then refilled my glass. "Thank you. You are a true friend."

"Tell you what," I said. "I've got my share of sad stories, even if they can't beat yours. But somehow I think we owe it to ourselves to put all those stories away for right now and concentrate on having a good time. What do you say?"

"I would like that."

"Good." I raised my drink. "How about if we get drunk? When's the last time you let yourself get rip-roaring drunk, huh?"

"A long time ago," she admitted. "It is another sad story, though."

"Then we won't talk about it," I said amiably. "And never fear. If there is one thing I've mastered during my brief stay on this planet, it's the art of a happy drunk."

"I don't know, James. . . ."

I raised the bottle from the ice bucket. It was still more than half full. I picked up the bucket and held out my free arm, taking on an officious voice. "The terrace awaits us, my dear, filled with surprises aplenty. Cheerful inebriation, the breath of the sea, romance lurking in the heavens, waiting to fall on those who dare look its way. Shall we?"

She linked her arm in mine, smiling radiantly. "I would be delighted, kind sir."

And so we proceeded to the terrace just outside her bedroom. I was already feeling the wine, and I could tell Marie had ventured close to the range of her tolerance. After setting the bucket down, I stood beside her and we looked out at the inky vastness surrounding the ship.

"I heard the captain say during dinner that we are moving into a storm," Marie said, taking a deep breath. "I can almost sense it coming. Can't you?"

I sniffed, darting my head about like a bloodhound onto a fresh scent. Marie giggled, then put her fingers to her lips. I moved closer to her, still sniffing, then nuzzled the tip of my nose behind her ear.

"Mmmmmmmmmm," I murmured. "Some storm."

"Oooh, that tickles!" She squirmed closer to me, slowly turning her face until our lips met. She gave me a short, searching kiss, then pulled herself gently away from me. "Mmmmmm," she purred back. "I liked that."

"I'm glad you did. The feeling was mutual."

She reached for her drink and after taking a sip she held it in front of her, almost like a barrier. "Tell me a funny story, James."

"It'll cost you another kiss," I bartered.

"Tell me the story first," she said slyly. "If it is a good one, it might be worth two kisses. Tell me a story about your golfing."

"A funny story about my golfing," I thought aloud, searching back through my memories. The first thing that came to mind was Kathleen and I making love on the fifth hole at the golf course in Australia. I quickly moved on to another time.

"The first job I ever had was working as a caddy at the ritziest country club in town," I began. "Me and my buddies would carry clubs around for all the local bigshots and really kiss up to them so we'd make good tips, then we'd turn right around and spend the money on clothes and cologne and whatever else we thought would help us be able to put the moves on their daughters, who usually hung out at the country club pool wearing skimpy bathing suits, trying to see how frustrated they could make us when we stopped by to get lunch at the grill next to the pool.

"One of the other fringe benefits of working at the club was that us caddies got to golf for free on Mondays, when the course was closed to everyone else while they mowed, fixed sprinklers and did all that other groundskeeping work they couldn't do the rest of the week. I usually played all day long, which helped my game a lot, believe me.

"Well, one Monday I stopped over at the grill to have a quick burger before I started playing my last nine holes of the day. It was kind of an overcast day, so there weren't that many people at the pool. But one of those people was Trina Valdez, this hot little number that all the caddies bragged about having had sex with, even though I knew they were all lying. Like me, they were all full of wishful thinking. Or so I thought. I was sitting there finishing my burger when she came over and started telling me how bored she was because none of her friends were at the pool and her dad, who happened to be Chairman of the Board of the club, was tied up at a meeting in the clubhouse and wasn't going to be able to take her home for another hour or so.

"Now, I'd been up nights many a time thinking over grand plans about how I was going to get my hands on Trina Valdez, and even though I was freaking out at my good luck, I managed to keep calm and suggest that I take her to a lookout point just off the thirteenth hole, where it was possible to see the lot next to the golf course, where some people were shooting a movie about aliens from outer space. Remember, this was twenty-five years ago, back in the late fifties, before there were any real sophisticated special effects. For this movie they had guys in wetsuits with nylons pulled over their heads playing monsters from outer space.

"Of course Trina was excited about the chance to see the filming, so I didn't have any trouble convincing her to come along with me. I had a lot of clout with the golf pro there, so I was able to get a golf cart, and we hightailed it straight over to the thirteenth hole, which was also the trickiest hole on the course. The green was set up on a hill surrounded by sandtraps and a long pond that wrapped itself around the base of the hill, almost like a moat. If you drove the cart up and around the edge of the green, there was a big thicket and a few trees. I drove between the thicket and trees until we came to a spot where we could see down the other side of the hill without anyone being able to see us. Clever me, eh?"

I looked to see if she was paying attention. She was. Her hand reached out and roamed up my back, then settled at the base of my neck, where she started playing with my hair as she listened. "Go on," she said.

I turned and kissed the back of her hand, then went on, "Of course, by this time it was after six and they'd finished shooting for the day, so there was nothing to see down the hill except the facade for a spaceship and a few parked jeeps that would probably represent the military transport for the Marines that would save Earth from the aliens in the last two minutes of the movie. I pretended to be disappointed and apologized to Trina. But, to my surprise, I assure you, she said she was glad.

"To make a long story short, she started seducing me . . . not that I needed much seducing. We kissed and kissed some more, just having a great old time, trying to make ourselves comfortable in this golf cart, right?"

"Oh no," Marie giggled, "Did the brake come loose?"

"How did you know?" I stared at her with disbelief.

"I'm right? I was just guessing."

"Well, you almost guessed it. Actually, I didn't even have the brake on. What's more, I was so nervous I hadn't even bothered to put the cart in gear when I turned it off. We were in neutral, and when we started moving around, the cart started rolling backwards the way we'd come."

"Oh no!" Marie laughed again.

"We rolled right across the green and over the flag," I said, laughing myself as the memory came back. "I was completely turned around in my seat, and by the time I got over my panic and tried to get my foot on the break, it was too late. Kersplash!"

"You went into the pond?" Marie was almost in hysterics. I could barely go on, I was laughing so much.

"Me and her and the cart. She ended up breaking her ankle and I chipped these two teeth." I pointed inside my mouth. "The cart was never the same. Neither was my job, needless to say."

We continued to laugh together. During the telling, we'd both managed to finish our wine. I hoped she was feeling as good as I was. She sure seemed to be.

"A funny story," she said. "That is such a funny story." Her eyes were dreamy.

"How funny?" I teased, tapping a finger against my lips.

She moved closer to me, reaching up and putting her hands back around my neck. Closing her eyes, she leaned forward tentatively, tilting her head back. I met her lips and we kissed, long and slow. She drew closer still, and I put my arms around her. As our bodies brushed against one another, she moaned slightly, letting out a sigh of air. "Very funny," she whispered, flicking the tip of her tongue lightly against my cheek. "Very, very funny."

We kissed again, and I carefully guided us back into her room. We were like Siamese twins connected by the lips, holding the kiss as she pulled my jacket off and flung it to one side. When our lips parted we looked at one another. Her eyes were filled with desire and longing.

"Here it is," I said with mock bravado, "the moment we've all been waiting for." I started unbuttoning my shirt from the middle. "Don't worry, I'll be gentle." I ripped my shirt open with a fierce jerk of both hands, sending buttons flying around the room.

Marie squealed with surprise and I laughed as I eased her back onto the bed and laid on top of her. We found each other's lips again. I could taste the sweetness of her breath through the wine.

"You surprised me," she snickered between kisses. "I was not expecting that."

"I'm full of surprises," I murmured, kissing her chin, then her neck. Her fingers stroked my chest and she moved her body slowly back and forth, encouraging my lips to explore more of her. What a creature she was. Seeming years of repressed desires boiled to the surface of her skin in prickles of gooseflesh wherever I touched her. Her own fingers swept across me in soft, tender flourishes, occasionally gathering together to pinch me lightly, then go on roving again. Somehow in the midst of the stroking we found our way out of our clothes—hadn't they melted away?—and we made love to the groan of distant rafters and the stirring of the even-more-distant sea. It was almost magical the way we took and gave as if we'd known each other's needs from years of togetherness. Her laughter gave way to pleasured moans, frantic, joyous tears and the teeth-gritting seethe of ecstacy when we came in unison. I'm sure I matched her sounds with some of my own. My God, was she fantastic!

When it was over, we had made an almost complete circle and were now facing the foot of the bed, our legs sprawled in all directions, our flesh still touching. Neither of us spoke.

Only a few minutes passed, but when I stirred and awoke with the familiar throbbing in my head, it seemed as if our partying and love-making had ended a long time ago. I slowly sat up and looked down at Marie. She was still asleep next to me, with a soft smile on her face.

I'm not a disciple or fan of psychology, so I can't account for the phenomenon of post-coital depression. Maybe it has something to do with the fact that love-making takes place within an aura of such intensity and focused reality that, in the wake of its aftermath, you inevitably feel let down to find yourself back in the everyday world and its beckoning list of concerns. Sorry, folks, but the ride is over. Please exit to your right and watch your step.

I went to the bathroom, then quietly started to dress. I was miserable. The more I thought about what I'd done, the worse I felt.

"James. . . ?" Marie was leaning on one elbow, watching me from the bed, still naked, her hair mussed. She had a worried look on her face.

"I have to go," I said, stepping into my pants.

"Your children?" she said, pulling the covers up around her. She smiled faintly. "I understand."

"I don't think so."

"What is it, James? Come here. Tell me."

I didn't think I could. I picked up my shirt from the floor and put it on, even though I couldn't button it back up. Marie got up from the bed and came over to me, hugging me from behind. I stepped away from her.

"Marie, I . . ." I looked at her. She was slipping into her housecoat. The worry was gone from her eyes now, replaced by the onset of hurt and confusion.

"If I wasn't good, I'm sorry," she whispered. "It's just that it's been so long since I've been with a man—"

"No, no, Marie, it's not that," I assured her. "You were incredible."

"Then I don't understand . . ."

I took a deep breath. I had to tell her. I owed her that much. "Marie, that story I told you . . . the golf story? Well, there was no Trina Valdez. It all happened the way I said, but the girl was Kathleen, my wife. It was the first time we were ever together. . . . And when we were making love, she . . . I kept picturing her. I wasn't trying to. You have to believe that. It's just that . . . five years . . . It's been five years since I've made love with her and . . . is any of this making any sense?"

Marie nodded, sitting back on the edge of the bed.

"Your wife," she said quietly. "You are still in love with her, yes?"

I didn't answer her.

"And she is married to another man now," she guessed.

"Yeah," I muttered. "Four years."

"And so you feel that you used me."

"I didn't mean to. It didn't start out like that at—"

"James," she interrupted, motioning for me to sit beside her. I did, and she cradled my chin in the palm of her hand. "You forget that I was the one who came to you on the deck tonight. I will not lie to you, either. When I came onto this boat, I knew that I would have to have a man, to know again what it was like to be held and kissed and made love to. I was in the disco looking for someone. I watched all the men in the ballroom during the ventriloquist's show, wondering how they would look with their clothes off, how they would feel next to me. Do you remember me looking at you? You were the one I liked best. And after we talked the next day, I knew I wanted you. So, you see, I used you, too. You filled my needs." She leaned forward and kissed me. "You made me feel like a woman again. I had a marvelous time."

"So did I," I admitted.

"Then what is there to feel guilty about? Why destroy such a special time?"

I shook my head, slightly dazed. "You're unreal, you know that, Marie?"

She smiled. "*Mon ami?*"

I furrowed my brow.

"My friend," she said. "Will you be my friend?"

"*Oui,*" I told her. "*Tres bien ami.*"

"Good."

"I *do* have to go."

She nodded, then laughed, "How will you explain your shirt?"

I looked down at my exposed chest, then bulged out my stomach and patted it. "The food."

We kissed and I went to the door. As I was on my way out, she called out, "James . . . ?"

I looked back.

"Thank you," she whispered.

"Thank *you*," I replied.

CHAPTER SIXTEEN

We were into the storm by morning. A downpour fell from gray skies and the waves were whipped up by the wind. It looked like it would last for at least the rest of the day.

Tilde had left a note under my door before the kids had retired, saying that their mother hadn't been home when they had called but that Rodessa had said everything was fine except for the weather. It was raining back in New York, too. What I noticed most about the note, though, was that Tilde hadn't even bothered to sign it. I knew her handwriting because it so closely resembled her mother's. It appeared that the Cold War was still on between us. I was in a good mood, having slept soundly after returning to my cabin last night. I decided that I owed the kids an apology for my outburst . . . and for a lot of other things.

I'd figured out that the reason things were screwed up on this trip was that I hadn't taken the time to sit down and talk to the kids about my feelings and about the change I hoped I had gone through. Instead, I had acted on the assumption that if I just carried on as if I were a new man, everything else would fall into place. Naive thinking, to be sure.

After showering and slipping into a shirt with all its buttons on, I ventured out of my room, ready to negotiate peace. I knocked on Tilde and Truman-Paul's room first. No answer.

"Tilde, Truman-Paul? Can we talk?"

I opened the door and looked in. They were gone. So was Trung. I went for breakfast, thinking I'd run into them there. One of the porters informed me that they'd eaten an hour ago and left. I sat down and had my coffee and morning paper, but I found myself missing their obnoxious presence.

To my amazement, by the time I finished breakfast, the storm was already showing signs of letting up. Only a slight drizzle was falling on the ship, so I went out and walked the decks by myself. Last night's encounter with Marie had left me in a romantic, introspective mood, a state I rarely find myself in. To anyone watching, I probably could have passed for a beardless Rod McKuen mulling over his next batch of poetic drivel. I did a lot of thinking, trying to sort through the clutter and crap I'd accumulated over the years and make some sense of my life. It was already becoming clear to me that a basic selfishness lay at the heart of most of my problems, but I thought if I scratched even deeper I'd find something even more fundamental.

As I was strolling past the ballroom, I heard the faint sound of a piano being played. I slowed down, recognizing the strains of Mozart. I peered in the window and saw Tilde sitting at the piano, her back turned to me, playing her half of the four-handed duet she always played for me with her mother whenever I visited them back in New York. I moved forward so that I could get a glimpse of her face, and was moved by her look of concentration as she watched her fingers. In four years she would be the same age as Kathleen when I first started dating her. It didn't seem possible.

Trung and Truman-Paul were off to one side, playing cards at the edge of the bandstand. They had the whole ballroom to themselves. I was about to go in and join them, but I held back and just watched them. I felt love for them, but also a tinge of envy, and I knew I was onto that fundamental key to what made James Paul Tannen tick.

James Paul Tannen didn't want to grow up.

There it was. A lifetime devoted to avoiding or shirking responsibility in hope of clinging to the carefree innocence of a child. Call me Peter Pan Tannen, perennial Boy Wonder, the precocious delinquent you can't help but feel for. I'll disarm you with charm, amaze you with youthful vigor, make you smile inside and wish you could be more like me. Yes, that was my scam. I was approaching forty and still living my life as if it were one constant summer vacation. And it hadn't been easy. Sacrifices had to be made. I'd given up my wife and family for starters. . . .

Instead of going inside, I backtracked from the ballroom before the children had a chance to see me, then went to the gift shop to buy a stationery pad and an airmail envelope. There were some things I wanted to put down on paper before they slipped away. Rushing back to my room, I pulled over my desk so that it faced out the window, then wrote to the beating of the rain. Letters have never been my strong suit, and as a rule I'll always call someone rather than write them. So the words came slowly. But they came.

By the time I'd finished, my wrist ached from writing and I'd filled five pages on the notepad. Outside, the rain had let up, so I decided to go back out on deck and read the letter over to make sure it made sense.

Dear Kathleen,
I am writing to you because you are the only person in the world who I have my children in common with, and the only person who knows me well enough so that my admissions of failure will come as no surprise.

Staff crewmen were already out, sweeping and mopping the decks where puddles had gathered. A few passengers stood in doorways, looking out at the sky, which was already beginning to clear.

I'm afraid you were right, Kathleen. I don't really have what it takes to be an integral (sp?) part of their lives. I guess I'm more like an "uncle" than a father to them. Lovable at a distance. Close up, I just can't seem to do anything right.

A steward's voice came over the public address system. After conveying a message in German and Swedish, he confirmed in English that we were now in the Mediterranean and that if the skies continued to clear we might be able to see Sardinia by mid-afternoon, our first sight of land since leaving the harbor in New York.

How odd it is to find myself speaking so intimately with you . . . feeling so close. I suppose it has to do with being with them. They remind me so much of you. Tilde, who has your strong, no-nonsense nature. Truman-Paul, who's every bit as frightened as the deepest, softest parts of you. And Trung, whose very presence serves as a reminder of the belief we both once had in Santa Claus, the Tooth Fairy, and the basic rightness of anything the two of us decided to do.

I went to the railing and looked out, spotting a gull shriek its joyous way along in air current, wings outstretched and head pointing sleekly forward. I defy anyone to take a close look at a bird in motion and not be overcome by a yearning ache to fly.

I miss you, Kathy. Dear Jesus, I do. That's why it's so hard to be with them. If a man can spend time alone with his children, it seems cruel that he has to be deprived of that same privilege with the woman who bore them. What I wouldn't give for a chance to turn the clock back ten years and—

"Dad?"

I almost dropped the letter over the railing. I turned around and saw the three kids standing together on the steps leading down from the ballroom entrance. Tilde was acting as spokesperson this time.

"We've talked things over and decided we're going to try to do better. We're going to be more considerate, if we can."

I studied their faces. They were downhearted and apprehensive, a hint of pleading in their eyes. I walked slowly toward them, folding my letter and sticking it in my back pocket.

"I've got an idea," I told them, sitting down on the steps and gesturing for them to join me. I hadn't had a chance to think through what I wanted to say, but when the timing's right a person has to wing it as best he can. "What if we thought of each other as friends? Friends."

I could see they were confused, so I went on, "You know what you have to do to keep a friend? You have to be nice to him. That goes for me as well as it goes for you. Considerate, like you said, Tilde." It sounded like it was coming out right. Might as well go for all the marbles. "Let's forget this 'father' stuff. I don't know how to do that. It only gets us in trouble. All I know is we've gotta do something different here or we'll never make it through the trip."

Their expressions changed. They seemed to be digesting it all, trying to get used to the idea. I liked it. It seemed like the right frame of mind to start working on a new and better relationship.

"Why don't you guys call me 'J.P.'? Hmmm? Why don't you try that on for size?" They were hesitant. I forged on, "I mean, what's greater than friendship, huh? That's what makes the world go-round. Come on, you guys, I think we've got a bead on this. From now on we're four friends takin' a vacation together, that's all. Just four friends on vacation. No big deal, and we're out to have the best time we've ever had!" I clapped my hands, excited about the idea. "What do you think?"

There was a moment of silence. The kids looked at one another, not sure how to react. Truman-Paul finally mustered, "I think it's nice . . . Jim."

I grinned and patted him on the back. "Hey, J.P. to my friends."

I looked at Trung. "Okay, J.P.," he said.

"Okay, J.P.," Tilde repeated.

It was a little awkward, granted. But I was sure we'd get used to it. I stood up, rubbing my hands together. "Okay! We're back on our feet again!"

CHAPTER SEVENTEEN

We spent the rest of the day getting used to the new arrangement. It all seemed forced at first, because we were all overly aware of the situation and it dominated everything we did. I was constantly correcting the kids when they called me Dad, and there was more than one occasion when I had to hold my tongue instead of imposing myself on them in a parental sort of way, like pointing out bad manners at the dinner table or making sure they brushed their teeth after we ate.

There was an artificiality to it all, but I hoped that if we over-reacted initially and then adjusted as we went along, we would stand a better chance of making a real change. Too much time had already slipped by to get bogged down taking baby steps.

After dinner, we retired to my cabin and poured over the travel pamphlets and maps of Rome. We were going to be docking near there for a daylong stopover, and I wanted us to reach a consensus intinerary so we could make the best of our time ashore. I'd traveled enough with the children before to know that lack of preparation only made for days filled with petty arguments and rampant indecision. It wasn't something we needed. Fortunately, we all wanted to see the same places—St.

Peter's, the Coliseum, the Roman Forum, and the Pantheon. With that settled, I suggested we turn in early and get a good night's sleep. There was a bit of uneasiness as we wished each other good night. I was almost ready to renege on our arrangement and put them each to bed and tell them good night after a kiss on the forehead, the way I usually did. But we had our pact. I got three waves and three " 'Night, J.P."s, then they were out the door and retiring to their own rooms.

I kicked off my shoes and sat back on the bed with my clothes on, staring at the ceiling. Was I doing the right thing here? It was so hard to tell. When a person gets fed up with himself, the first thing he loses confidence in is his instincts. I was tempted to track down Marie and tell her what had happened. I would have trusted her opinion. But it didn't seem right. I'd already slipped her a note thanking her again for the previous night. If I went back another time it might be taken the wrong way.

I took out the letter I'd written to Kathleen, thinking I might add onto it. But it occurred to me that even if I sent the letter out as soon as we reached Rome, there was a chance I'd be seeing her again before it even reached her. That's one of the inadequacies of correspondence. You mail your thoughts one day and by the time they're read by someone else you might be in a completely different frame of mind. I finally tore up the letter and tossed it in the wastebasket. Kathleen had asked that I respect her happiness. The only thing I could hope to accomplish with the letter was to disrupt that happiness on the slim chance that I could follow up and take advantage of the confusion. There might have been a time when such a maneuver would have been right up my alley, but I was trying to get away from those Typical Tannen Moves.

I didn't sleep well that night, and when I woke up there were still images lingering from the dreams that had kept me tossing and turning. I'd taken Marie for a ride in a golf cart and we'd wound up watching from cover as Mitchell and Kathleen made love on a putting green. I think part of the same dream had me at a golf range, driving golf balls as hard as I could at my children while they tried to keep from being hit. They were laughing like it was a game until one of the balls had struck Truman-Paul on the head and sent him falling to the ground with blood streaming from his forehead.

In the dream that had woken me up, I'd found myself on the promenade deck of the ship, leaning over the railing and looking down at the sea when someone had come up behind me and pushed me overboard. I'd fallen swiftly, beating my arms like I was trying to fly right up to the moment that I hit the water.

We hadn't been able to see Sardinia the previous afternoon, so when I looked out my window and saw the coast of Italy near Rome, the sight was uplifting enough to chase away the flutters of anxiety from my dreams. I dressed quickly and was putting my shoes on when there was a knock on my door and the kids came in, already suited up and ready for breakfast. They were all wearing the clothes I'd bought for them back in Los Angeles.

"Morning, J.P.!" Truman-Paul said, doffing his sailor's cap.

"Hey, come on, you guys," I told them. "You don't have to do that just for me. Beside, you don't want to wear those things ashore. It's apt to be dirty and—"

"We just thought we'd do it for breakfast," Tilde said. "To please you."

"Oh yeah? Well, in that case, let's go," I said, joining them. "And let me tell you, I *am* pleased. Very much. In fact, I'm so pleased that I'm not even going to drink coffee *or* look at a newspaper at the table. What do you think of that?"

"Yay!" Truman-Paul said.

"Can I bring my game?" Trung asked. When I glanced at him, he laughed. "Just kidding."

We ate quickly, because the ship was coming into the harbor and the kids wanted to be out on the deck to see the ship dock. Ours was easily the biggest ship in the port, so we are able to see the whole operation, which took close to an hour. When the voice over the intercom told passengers that they would be able to leave the ship shortly, we went back to our rooms and quickly changed into casual clothes.

The kids were excited and made a nuisance of themselves pushing through the throng of passengers making their way down the steep incline of the ramp, leading down from the ship. I offered apologies in their wake. Just as he was about to reach the docks, Truman-Paul tripped on a raised plank and fell forward onto all fours. It had taken him by surprise and I could see that he was about to cry. I moved in and wisked him back up to his feet, then brushed him off as the crowd streamed around us.

"Cherrio, old chap," I told him with a clipped British accent. "Small spill. No harm done, now. As you were. Arms up, chest out, breathe deep, chin up. Don't forget the chin up, old chap." Truman-Paul lost his tears to a burst of laughter and we all fell in together as we headed down the dock for shore. I was practically dancing alongside them, I was feeling so good.

"Okay, guys. One thing to remember. All roads might lead to Rome, but once they get there they wander all over the place, so we have to stick together or we'll end up lost. I don't want to have to barter with gypsies to get any of you back, got it?"

"Sure thing, J.P.!" Truman-Paul said, gawking at the bevy of peddlers who had converged upon the docks to make their bids for fresh tourist lira. I paused and swerved to one side, having spotted Marie amidst a group of passengers boarding a tourist bus with their luggage.

"Hello!" I called out, getting her attention.

"Hello," she said with a smile, taking in the children.

"Marie, I'd like you to meet three close friends of mine," I said, doing introductions. "This is Truman-Paul, and Tilde . . . and this here's Trung. Gang, this is Marie, a *very* nice person."

They exchanged greetings. I looked at the luggage she was carrying, then said, "We're spending the day in Rome. Want to come along?"

She shook her head, still smiling. "Our group is going to Naples, then on around the southern tip of Italy." Noticing the shift in my expression, she added, "We catch up with the ship in Athens."

"Oh," I said, a little disappointed. "Well, have fun."

"You too." To the others, she said, "It's nice to meet you."

She vanished inside the bus and we moved on. Tilde was immediately up to her old tricks. "You two certainly seemed friendly," she said.

"Yeah, well, she's a nice lady."

"When did you get so *friendly*?"

I curled my thumb and index finger into a make-believe monocle and pressed it against one eye as I squinted at Tilde. "And vaht about *you*? Ven did *you* get so friendly?" I pinched her slightly in the ribs and she laughed.

There was a row of taxis lined up along the curb once we cleared the docks. I looked for the one with the least dents, ignoring the pitches from the dozen other drivers waving fingers indicating for how few lira I could place our lives in their hands. I'd been to Rome twice before, and no matter how many jokes you hear about Italian drivers, they only scratch the surface. We weren't more than two blocks from port when our driver almost gave us a tour of the front end of a school bus coming the other way. I groaned as I reached for the kids, and the driver merely grinned as he jerked the steering wheel to one side and missed a collision by inches. He waved away the close call, as well as my request that he pick a lane, any lane, and stick to it. We went a few more blocks before I had him drop us off at a corner near Hadrian's Tomb so we could switch over to a less threatening mode of transport. Following a trail of horse-droppings, we reached a spot where we could board a carriage bound for St. Peter's.

"Look at all the people!" Truman-Paul said, staring at the throngs crowding the street all around us.

"That's nothing, Truman," I told him. "You should see this place on Sunday! Sometimes there's a *million* of them all crowded together in the square to hear the Pope."

"Wow!"

Tilde said, "Mom once told us that when she came here with you, you got thrown out of one of the museums because you took off your shirt and tried to pose next to a statue."

"She told you that?" I asked, surprised. I'd been drunk that time, and she'd dared me to do it, sure that I wouldn't. I'd shown her. It had turned into our first big fight of that particular trip. It was weeks later before she could laugh at it.

"I think you should try it again," Trung said. "I could take a picture."

"Not on your life," I told him. "And don't let me catch you trying it, either."

We got out of the carriage just outside the square, but never made it inside the church because the kids wanted to watch the food vendors working the nearest side street. There was a family turning out peanut brittle from scratch with assemblyline precision, taffy pullers nimbly stretching large wads of goo, and at least five one-man operations selling roasted chestnuts by the coneful. We sampled some of everything until even Truman-Paul's sweet tooth had been satisfied.

"Okay, let's walk a few pounds of this off, guys," I finally suggested, taking off my jacket and slinging it over my shoulder like some local *bravagente* as I started swaggering down the sidewalk. I told Trung and

Truman-Paul, "Now, to look Italian, you walk-a like-a this, see? Like in-a the movies, you ain't gonna look a-right or left. Straight ahead, like-a you own the world."

Truman-Paul fell in beside me, seriously trying to copy my walk. Trung took up the other side, but he was deliberately making fun of me, exaggerating his movements so that he looked like a wind-up toy with a faulty spring.

"That's not-a bad, a-Trung," I said with a straight face. "You're a-doing fine, too, Truman. 'ey, a-Tilde, how do we look? Wathchoo think, 'ey?"

She rolled her eyes at us, keeping her distance. "I think I don't know any of you."

"Aye!" I grinned at the boys as we kept walking, drawing stares. "She don't *a-know* us!"

Trung laughed, "That's a-too bad."

"Yeah," Truman-Paul cried out. "Mamma Mia!"

Tilde followed a few steps behind us, her arms crossed in front of her. "Why do you have to look *Italian*?"

"Someone very famous once said 'When in Rome, do as the Romans do,'" I explained, slowing down and pointing to a nearby magazine stand, where two men stood, their backs turned to us. "Look, see those guys? Now, those are real items. Bonafide natives. Observe the natives and you get to know the country much faster. Come on . . ."

As we started to walk toward them, the two men turned away from the stand and smiled with recognition. They were the two Hungarian twins from the ship. Tilde snickered as I nodded a greeting to the men and they walked off.

" 'Bonafide natives,' " she taunted.

"Well, Hungary is very close to Italy, Tilde. Some of their customs are very similar."

"I want to see some ruins!" Truman-Paul said.

"Yeah, let's go to the Coliseum," Trung said.

We turned off Via della Conciliazione and started down one of the side streets leading to the bridge cross-

ing the River Tevere, which was brown with silt and
looked like flowing chocolate milk. As we approached
the bridge, a family of ragged-clothed gypsies drifted
across the street towards us.

"Oh, oh," I muttered. "Hurry up, guys."

The gypsies were quickly upon us, holding their
hands out and pleading in rapid-fire Italian. There was
a mother, grandmother, and five children, all under ten,
all talking at once, all staring at us with wide, dark eyes.
Truman-Paul clung to me, terrified, and Tilde just
watched them, uncomprehending. Trung, however, became enraged. He started pushing the gypsies away,
cursing them in Filipino. I led Tilde and Truman-Paul
clear of the altercation, and finally the gypsies fled
down the street, making their way towards another clot
of tourists.

Trung was still seething when he rejoined us.

"You didn't have to be so rough with them," Tilde
scolded.

"What do you know about it?" Trung snapped.

"That's enough, Trung," I said. "Let's go catch a
bus."

"Who were they?" Truman-Paul said, trembling, as
we crossed the bridge to Corso Vittorio Emmanuel.

"Gypsies," I told him.

"They're poor people," Tilde said, still looking at
Trung. "They were just begging. They were probably
hungry."

"They're thieves!" Trung snapped. "They come up
close and poke at you like they're begging, but if they
can get their hands in your pockets they'll steal whatever's there."

"That's a terrible thing to say!" Tilde said with alarm.

"It's true!"

I moved over and put an arm around Trung. "Hey,
easy, Trung."

"I know it!" he shouted, glaring at Tilde. "She doesn't
know anything about it!"

"All right, all right." I took Trung aside and lowered my voice. "I know you know, Trung. Tilde doesn't understand, but don't get on her case about it, okay?"

He looked over my shoulder at her. "She's never been hungry. She's never had to live out on the streets—"

"Drop it, Trung," I told him firmly. "Leave it be. Do yourself a favor. It's behind you."

He calmed down a little, but I could still see that he was upset. He finally muttered. "Sometimes I think I belong out here with them, that's all."

"I understand, Trung," I told him. "I understand. Now come on, let's not let it spoil things, okay? Try to get over it."

He shrugged his shoulders and we crossed the street to the pickup spot where a line of buses was idling, belching black smoke from their exhaust pipes. I stayed between Trung and Tilde, watching him look out at the street urchins hanging out in alleys and at corners. I doubted that he'd ever get over it.

CHAPTER EIGHTEEN

Tilde had figured out the reason for Trung's outburst and she apologized to him while we were taking the bus to the Coliseum. But the mood amongst our once-merry band had been brought down a few notches. We were in need of some comic relief, and when the situation calls for someone to make a fool of himself, there's no more able candidate than James Paul Tannen.

Once we were inside the weather-eaten framework of the Coliseum, I played the role of energetic tour guide, gesturing profusely as I gave my play-by-play recreation of the arena's tainted past. I tried not to let the facts get in the way of a good story.

". . . and, listen, if you think there's a big rivalry these days between the Dodgers and the Giants, well, you should have been here when this joint first opened for business. I'm telling you, back then it was the Lions against the Christians, playing before packed houses . . . and this was before they had Fan Appreciation Days or baseball cap giveaways, mind you. Just picture it; thousands of Romans crowding the benches, drinking beers on a hot afternoon and getting rowdy waiting for the big showdown. Up there in the box seats you'd have Julius Caesar trying to impress Cleopatra 'cause maybe he wants to unload some overpaid gladiator on her, in trade for a future draft choice or something.

"Well, once things are ready, the Christians come out and everybody boos, because they're the visiting team. These Romans are real Lions fans, I'm tellin' ya."

"How crude," Tilde complained.

"Hush," I told her. Truman-Paul was listening to me with wide-eyes and even Trung was mildly enjoying himself now. "Anyway, out come the Lions, and the crowd just roars because they love 'em so much. Pretty soon there's plenty of action, tooth and fang, prayer and paw. One of the Lions gets a Christian down, then looks up to Julius Caesar and waits for the signal. If it's thumbs up, the Christian's lucky. But if it's thumbs down, oh-oh, that poor guy is history. I mean, down for the ten count . . ."

Truman-Paul interrupted, "How did the Lion know to look up and wait for a signal?"

I looked at him incredulously. "Don't be so smart, asking questions like that, Truman-Paul. How are you going to learn anything if you expect me to make sense?!"

"It was the gladiators who looked to Caesar, Dad," Tilde enlightened me.

"Big deal," I sniffed. "Big hairy difference."

They teamed up to give me a hard time. "Yeah, big deal." Truman-Paul laughed.

"Big hairy difference," Trung mocked.

"I called you Dad," Tilde remembered. "Sorry, J.P."

"Hey, listen, you just call me whatever's comfortable, okay?" I leered playfully at Trung. "Within reason, of course."

The ruins of the Forum were right across the street, so we had just enough time to take them in. As we walked amongst the toppled columns and pedestals of aged stone, I told the kids, "When I was back in high school, I made a model of these ruins for a history project. What I did was fill a big bowl with green clay, then I took our Monopoly game and painted out the green houses white so they'd look like temples, sort of. I pushed golf tees into the clay upside down to make columns and obelisks, and for trees I dipped q-tips into green food coloring. Boy, you should have seen it when I was finished with it. It was a work of art . . . garbage." I broke out laughing at the memory. "God, it was so ugly my teacher said there was probably people rolling over in their catacombs at the mere thought of it."

Adjacent to the Forum ruins were those of Palantine Hill, which were condos of a sort for the Roman hierarchy in their heyday. Atop the hill was a large garden, and I pleaded fatigue so I could grab a bench and rest while the kids explored the grounds and had a tour of some of the building that had been more preserved than most.

I thought back to my trip here with Kathleen, which we'd made a year before Truman-Paul was born, to celebrate our third anniversary. We had left Tilde with her grandparents so that we could have some time to ourselves far away from home. The night before the day I'd been asked to leave the Basilica of St. Paul for impersonating a statue, we stayed on the grounds of Palantine Hill after they had chased the other tourists out and had closed for the night. We'd managed to sneak into one of the rooms formerly used by Julius Caesar and made love on a towel we'd lain over the intricate tile work of the floor. It had been rather painful on the knees—much worse than the fifth hole green back in Australia—but how often does one get to indulge oneself in the private chambers of a Roman Emperor. I ask you. I suppose it was the euphoria of that indiscretion that had prompted me to strike a Caesarean pose at the museum the next day. Looking back, I couldn't believe I had actually done it. But, then, as Kathleen would have put it, it was another Typical Tannen Move. Funny how you can go out of your way trying to be unique and unlike anyone else and then end up being caught up by your own predictability. Ah, life's sweet mysteries.

This was the last place Kathleen and I had made love somewhere besides a bedroom. Perhaps I should have contacted the people at Michelin about erecting a plaque! *James Paul Tannen and his loving wife Kathleen slept here, loved here, promised their hearts to each other forever here, under the watching eye of a full Roman moon on the occasion of their third wedding.*

"I'm hungry for pizza!" Truman-Paul gasped as he ran up to the bench.

"I want spaghetti," Tilde voted, coming up behind him.

"How about cheeseburgers?" Trung wanted to know.

I glanced at my watch. "How about if we get our butts back to the ship before it takes off without us? Then you can order whatever you like."

We were fortunate enough to find a cab driver with a wife and family to live for, and we made it back to the docks without incident, well before the ramp was pulled up and the ship was tugged out and sent on its way. The kids yawned their way through a dinner of pizza, spaghetti *and* cheeseburgers, and, for the first time, they shunned the dessert cart when it rolled by.

We went back to our cabins. After I brushed my teeth, I came back out to check on the kids. Trung was already in bed, but I could tell he wasn't asleep yet. He'd been quiet all through dinner and I was worried about him.

"Something's bothering you, Trung," I told him, sitting on the edge of the bed. "Is it the street people? The gypsies?"

"I'll be okay," he said, rolling over on his side. "I'm just tired. Long day."

I put a hand on his shoulder. "Okay, Trung. But if you ever feel like you have to talk about it, I'm here to listen."

"Thanks," he said.

"Good night, Trung." I stood up and went to the door.

" 'Night," He mumbled. As an afterthought, he added, "J.P."

Tilde and Truman-Paul wanted to hear a bedtime story. I hadn't heard them ask for one in years, so I took it as a good sign. I was exhausted, but there was no way I was going to turn them down.

"Scoot over, Truman." I laid down next to him while Tilde propped her head up in her bed to listen.

"Do you guys remember when I had you out last summer at my place, and we went for a ride back in the hills where there were hardly any houses?"

"Yeah," Truman-Paul said. "The boonies, right?"

"The one and same." I continued, "Well, your old man has his eyes on a nice big piece of property back in those hills. It's a valley, tucked away by itself, real privatelike. Now, you can imagine what it would be like to put some real nice houses there, down in the valley where they wouldn't spoil the view of people driving by the main roads? I'd build them in a big, wide circle, and right smack dab in the middle I'd put a golf course."

"You're kidding," Truman-Paul said.

"Hey, I never kid, Tru, you know that. Now be quiet and let me finish. It keeps getting better. Now think about it real hard and you'll see how beautiful it can be. Just imagine the way the shadows crawl across sandtraps when the sun gets low on the horizon. And the way the water holes kick up in a high wind. That's what you'd be able to see, right out your front window; a big picture window that looks out on the whole course, with its gently rolling hills, and flags flapping in the breeze. And the whole thing would be called . . . 'Village Green.' "

The kids took it in a few moments, then Truman-Paul asked me, "How do people get from their cars to their houses if they're surrounded by grass?"

I raised an eyebrow. I had that one figured out. "They park their cars in a community parking lot and drive a golf cart right to their front door."

Tilde said, "How do they keep golfballs from smashing their windows?"

I groaned and sank into the bed. Where was these kids' sense of romance?

Truman-Paul must have noticed my dismay. He shifted on the bed and started playing with the hairs on my chest, telling me earnestly, "It's a good idea, Jim."

The way he said my name struck me oddly. That hadn't been one of my more brilliant ideas, I thought. "Well, Truman," I said with visionary confidence, "I haven't worked out all the bugs yet, but people are going to love it, take my word." I snapped my fingers and craned my neck to see Tilde. "Special glass. The windows will be made of special glass!"

She still wasn't convinced. "People will have to wear helmets if they want to barbecue on the patio."

I let out a snort. "I think it's time for bed."

I leaned over and kissed Truman-Paul on the forehead.

"That's not how," he told me.

"No?"

"Like this." Truman-Paul pushed me down, then hovered over me, holding my face between his small hands. He kissed my forehead, then my eyelids, then the tip of my nose, then my chin, then both cheeks, and finally a loving peck on the lips. He must have been watching the Italians when I wasn't looking.

"Oh, Truman," I sighed, genuinely moved. "I'm floating."

I was giving him a hug when there was a knock on the door.

"Yes," I called out. "What is it?"

"Mister Tannen?" a steward called out.

"Yes?"

"You're wanted in the communications room."

CHAPTER NINETEEN

The communications room was like a mole's lair, cloaked in a darkness offset by the dim shaft of a low intensity light and the luminous glow of bulbs and gauges on control panels used to keep the ship in touch with land, and vice versa. When I entered the room and drifted over to the counter, a man on the other side swivelled around from his post before the switchboard, without taking his hands off the dials and toggles in front of him.

"It's from Athens," he told me, nodding toward a phone on the desk before me. "You can take it on that one there."

I nodded, still confused. Athens? I didn't know anyone in Athens. I thought of Marie, but quickly realized it would be days before her group reached there.

The phone's connection was terrible, and through the crackle of static and white noise I was only able to make out a faint male voice, sounding like someone was talking to me from the other side of a dream.

"Who?" I asked, pressing the phone closer to my ear. I looked back at the Communications Officer. "I can't hear."

He adjusted some controls and shifted his headphones

slightly so that they covered his ears better. When he glanced over his shoulder and looked at me questioningly, I raised a hand for him to stop. The voice was becoming clearer.

"What? Can you speak louder?" I said into the mouthpiece. There was a pause, followed by a brief gargle of more static, then the voice came in clearer. I was taken aback. "Mitchell? Is that you? Yes, this is Jim." I didn't get it. "You're in Athens? What are you doing in Greece?"

His voice wavered in and out of the crackling interference. I caught only a few words. One of them was *Kathleen*. The other was *accident*. I put a hand over my free ear and looked with frustration at the officer. He shrugged to indicate he was doing the best he could.

"You what?" I said to Mitchell. I'd been ready to fall asleep in seconds only a few minutes ago. Now adrenalin was coursing through me like a rampant jolt of electricity. "She what? I can't hear you clear . . ."

I heard him mention an accident again, then something about being sorry. All the energy running through me suddenly contracted into the pit of my stomach. I felt sick, but too numb to move. Words fell out of my mouth as the awful truth swept over me.

"Is she all right? . . . She *what*? . . . Mitchell, did you say. . . . Oh, no . . . Oh, God, please. . . . No."

Kathleen was dead.

Kathleen was dead.

Dead.

The scraps of words on the other end fell into place. Car crash . . . instantly . . . burial . . . the kids. I was barely listening. Every part of me was tightening inward, as if some outer force were trying to squeeze the life out of me and only coming up with tears.

On the other line, Mitchell was asking me a question.

"No, I . . ." I asked the officer for a pencil and paper. "Yes, Mitchell yes, I think . . . that's a good. . . ." I scribbled something down, then cupped my hand over the mouthpiece and asked the officer, "When do we get to Greece?"

"Thirteen hundred tomorrow," he said. "One o'clock."

I passed along the message. Mitchell's voice was fading out again. I leaned over, bracing myself against the counter to compensate for the weakness in my legs. A pained sob wrenched its way out of my mouth, shaking me with its brutal force. I swallowed hard to keep another one from following it out.

"What?" I wept into the receiver. "I see . . . of course . . . I know you couldn't, Mitchell . . . Yes, yes, I know you do . . . hello? . . . hello?"

I lowered the receiver, letting the garbled hiss escape into the room. "We lost each other," I mumbled to the officer. I closed my eyes, trying to deny the truth I couldn't. Kathleen was dead. I would never see her again.

"We lost each other," I said again.

CHAPTER TWENTY

I had to get away from everyone and be by myself. There was an isolated upper deck near the navigation chamber I remembered seeing the first day we explored the ship. It was supposed to be off-limits to passengers and I had to climb over a locked gate to reach it, but once I was there the rest of the ship fell from view and I knew no one could see me, either. I stared out, catching my breath. Miles away, there were barely detectable specks of winking light marking the coast of either Italy, Sardinia or Sicily. I wasn't sure which way I was facing or which way we were going. My only awareness was the sense of being alone, as alone as anyone could ever want, or not want, to be. Kathleen, I kept crying out inside. Kathleen, where are you? My mind was staging its last feeble defense against the news of her death. I tried to reject the fact, grasp for any explanation that would disavow it. Maybe I had heard Mitchell wrong. Maybe it hadn't been Mitchell on the phone at all. There had been so much distortion on the line it might have been anyone . . . maybe someone with a sick mind and a grudge I didn't know about. There were thousands of possibilities, I tried to tell myself. But deep down I knew they were all lies. Fooling myself wasn't going to bring her back. Nothing was going to. Once that became clear, I tortured myself with all the wasted opportunities I'd had to save her life. If only I hadn't taken the kids of this cruise, or if I'd picked them up at another time, Kathleen would have been with them and it wouldn't have happened. If I'd insisted that we all do something together. . . . If I'd have just stayed in Malibu and not bothered with this pipedream of coming back into my kids's lives. . . . If only I'd dedicated myself to being a decent husband and father in the first place. . . .

If, if, if. It didn't mean a thing now. Kathleen was dead, taken away from me. She'd waved her last good-byes to us back on the docks in New York. It was the last time I'd seen her, the last time I'd ever see her. She was already in the ground now; buried in an oak coffin that would only protect her disfigured remains so long before the wood rotted and the worms got to her.

"No!" I shouted defiantly into the night. I filled my lungs with air and screamed it again, as if I thought I might call down all the gods of Greece and Rome until I could find one who would give me Kathleen back. "NOOOOOOOOOOOOOOOOOO!"

We were too far out to sea for an echo, and the scream was swallowed by the night. A few moments later there were voices below and I heard footsteps approaching. Someone was starting to call up to me when someone else stopped them. The communications officer, no doubt, telling them to leave me alone. No one came up. I didn't come down. I stayed there on that desolate platform the rest of the night, trying to make sense of it all, trying to figure out where to go, what to do next. I began to wish it had been me that had died. It would have been more fitting, more justified. I'd centered my life around myself and my own selfish needs. My dying wouldn't have left a large gap in anyone's life, no major difference beyond a few days of grief and an occasional fond memory of those few times when I'd been a halfway decent human being. But Kathleen was loved and needed. She deserved to live. All that's good in the world was meant for people like her to enjoy and share with others like her. She had a right to see her children grow. She had a right to age with grace and serenity. When it was time for her to die, years and years from now, she had a right to go peacefully, surrounded by those close to her. It wasn't right that she had to die alone in the twisted wreckage of a car under some godforsaken concrete underpass in the rain. It wasn't right. It wasn't fair. . . .

I had no idea of the time that had passed until the eastern horizon began to take on a graying tinge. It was almost dawn.

The kids.

They would be up soon. I couldn't face them in my condition. What was I going to tell them? How? It was all I could do to make it back to my cabin without breaking down again. I scrawled a quick note and posted it outside my door, telling them that I'd come down sick during the night and needed to sleep. I collapsed in my bed and stared blankly out my window at the brightening day. Tears poured freely down my face and I did nothing to clear them away. My eyes began to sting. I was still awake when I heard the kids come out a half hour later and whisper to one another outside the door as they read the note. They left without knocking, but before they went for breakfast they slipped something under the door. I got up and found that they had made me a quick "get well" card. Tilde had done the lettering, Trung had contributed a border, and Truman-Paul had drawn stick figures of the three of them with round smiling faces. I took the card back to bed with me and kept looking at it until I finally fell asleep. I don't remember dreaming.

There was a knock on my door at noon.

"J.P.?" It was Trung. "We're almost to Greece. You okay?"

"Uh, yeah, much better," I said groggily. I felt miserable. "I'll be out in a bit. Why don't you guys just get yourselves ready to go ashore?"

"Aren't you coming?"

"I'll try my best," I said. "Thanks for the card."

"That's okay."

A shower helped things somewhat, but I was still feeling shaky. Whenever I thought about Kathleen, I could feel the tears start to come. I knew I wasn't going to be able to face them without the same thing happening. It wouldn't be right. They'd need someone to lean on, and I wanted to be ready to at least do that much for them.

I put a call through to Mandy, the Childrens' Activities Director. She'd been able to latch onto some beefcake lawyer after I'd turned down her advance at the bar earlier on the cruise, and she'd been cordial to me the few times we'd talked since. I asked her if she could give the kids a tour of the sights in Athens that afternoon. She put up a small stink about me giving her such short notice, but she apparently had no real plans and when I said I was sick she apologized for the flack and promised to do what she could. I poured myself a drink and laid down a few minutes with a cold washcloth over my eyes, which were puffed-up and bloodshot.

Tilde knocked this time and asked, "Dad, can we come in?"

I finished my drink and set it aside. "Yeah, okay."

When they walked in, Truman-Paul gasped, "How come you got your eyes covered like that, Dad? What happened."

"I'm having an allergic reaction to something," I lied, blowing my nose. I lowered the washcloth and looked at them, noticing them cringe slightly at the sight of me. "I look that bad, huh?"

"You look *awful*," Tilde said.

"Well, I feel that way, too, guys. Listen, I just talked

with the activities director, and she's going to show you around this afternoon."

"Is she the one with the tight pants?" Truman-Paul asked.

"No, Truman, she isn't," I told him. "She's the one we met when we first came on board. She's a nice person. You'll all have a good time."

"Aren't you coming ashore at all?" Tilde asked.

"I might, but just to see if I can find something for my allergies. I've already seen Athens before."

"With Mom?" Truman-Paul asked.

"That's right, Truman-Paul."

"Gee, you guys must have been *everywhere*."

"Not quite," I told him softly, trying to keep my voice from shaking. "Not quite."

"Don't worry, Dad," Trung said, standing taller than usual. "I'll keep an eye on us."

"You all keep an eye on each other," I advised them. "And don't give Mandy a hard time, okay?"

"It won't be as much fun without you coming along," Truman-Paul sulked.

"I'll be better for Egypt. I promise. Now go have a good time for me, and I'll see you tonight."

"What are you allergic to?" Tilde asked.

"I don't know, Tilde."

"Maybe it's a yeast infection," Truman-Paul suggested.

I had to laugh. "No, I don't think so."

"Dad? What was that message about last night?" Tilde said.

I nodded and looked at the kids, one by one. I took a deep breath, thinking it was time to tell them. But at the last minute I changed my mind and said, "They can take telegrams, too. It was just some business stuff my partners wanted me to know about."

"Good news or bad?" Trung asked.

The ship's horn sounded, coming to my rescue. I got to my feet and clapped my hands. "Okay, you guys. Go have fun and stay out of trouble. When you get back you can tell me all about it."

I shooed them out of the room, then leaned against the door, closing my eyes as I listened to them walk away, whispering back and forth.

"I bet it was bad news he found out about."

"You don't have allergic reaction to *news*, Trung."

"Maybe he doesn't really *have* an allergy, Tilde."

"What's that supposed to mean?"

"I don't know. . . ."

Truman-Paul said, "I hope he didn't get a curse at the ruins."

"What are you talking about, Truman-Paul?"

"Like the kind with King Tut. Remember when we saw that television show and they said the guys who found King Tut got hit with a curse that made them sick?"

"That's just television crap," Trung sneered.

"Don't say 'crap,' Trung. It's not nice."

"Who cares?"

I shook my head to myself and walked away from the door. Mandy was going to earn her wages today.

I went into the bathroom and started running water in the sink, then lathered up my face to shave. I *was* going ashore later, but not to find something to treat either an allergy or a curse.

Mitchell would be waiting there to see me.

CHAPTER TWENTY-ONE

We met at the Athens Hilton, where Mitchell was staying. Whenever and wherever Mitchell travels, you'll be able to find him at the Hilton, provided there's one there for him to stay at. Makes his itineraries less complicated, more efficient. More Mitchell-like.

He was wearing a white suit and toting a white Panama hat. His beard was neatly groomed and he seemed well composed. You'd have had to know him, and even then you would have had to sneak a deep look into his eyes to see where he was hiding his grief. I saw it while he was ordering drinks at the patio cafe where we decided to talk. I knew Mitchell enough to know he was taking refuge in his fastidiousness. Life had heaped chaos upon him; his best defense was order, control. It's his way. I envied him for it in a way. I was a wreck, holding myself together by mere threads of self-control.

". . . I'd gone to Detroit from Cleveland," he was telling me. "I'd just spoken to her to let her know where I was . . . but it was Friday, and I didn't bother to let my office know. It was almost three days before anyone found me." He coughed lightly, but I knew he was just bringing his voice under control. "I thought it was best to bury her . . . then come and break the news to the

146

children, bring them back . . . then have a memorial service."

Another reason I hadn't told the kids about their mother's death was that I had promised Mitchell I wouldn't until we met up with him. If I would have broken down and told them earlier, I would have either told Mitchell I had misunderstood him on the phone or I would have just told him it seemed best at the time and have left it at that. I stared past him at the Acropolis, which rose majestically in the distance, crowned with the ruins of Greece's ancient glory. Ant-sized tourists roamed the columns and facades. Somewhere there, Trung, Tilde and Truman-Paul were hopefully being given an informed-but-informal tour by Mandy.

"I hope you understand," Mitchell said, raising his voice slightly to draw my attention.

I nodded vaguely, only half-listening to him.

He leaned forward, fingering the rim of his hat as he spoke. "I've booked rooms for all of us at the hotel. I'd like to take the children off the ship tonight . . . fly them home in the morning. I have a room for you as well."

I turned my full attention to him suddenly, just beginning to understand what he was leading to.

"I've booked you right along with us to New York, with a ticket that goes on to California. But I'm hoping you'll stay with us a little while. I know the children would appreciate it. I would, too."

I picked up my drink and took a long sip, never taking my eyes off him.

"I spoke to a psychiatrist. He said they're going to need all the moral support they can get."

I set my drink back down slowly, trying not to betray the jackhammer surge of adrenalin that had my heart leaping against my ribcage. Easy, Tannen, I told myself. Easy.

Mitchell was taking a hard look at me. It was clear that he could read my thoughts as well as I could read his. He talked on, though, as if he was sure his eloquence would thwart the inevitable. "That's why I made this trip. On his advice. To give them the reassurance that life is going to go on. With the exception of this . . . this enormous loss . . . they need to know all things will remain equal."

So there it was. The bottom line. He underlined it. "There will still be their house to return to. Their rooms. Their friends. Their school. Their housekeeper, who's like a second mother to them . . . and so many more things that represent safety, and security, and stability." He stared at me, probing for a reaction. I held it back from him. I just stared back at him, saying nothing. "It's very important. That all things remain equal."

I picked up my drink and took another sip. It was Ouzo and ice water, strong with the taste of licorice, clear and cold, propping me up with its potency.

"So," Mitchell concluded, sitting back with an air of finality. He almost looked like he believed it was going to go down just like he'd planned it. Almost. His voice took on a guarded edge. "Why don't you come back to the hotel and clean up. We'll open up your room, then you can take a nap before we go and pick up. . . ."

He let the sentence hang, noticing that I was shaking my head.

"What is it, Jim?" He was leaning forward again, ready for what was coming.

"I'd like to be alone with them tonight," I told him with what passed for calmness under the circumstances.

He crossed his legs and stroked his moustache as he eyed me clinically. We were playing chess now, and I had the advantage on him. I was familiar with the way he was acting. He'd never seen me like this before. For once, I was being unpredictable.

"I don't think that's a very good idea," he finally said.

"I want to," I replied matter-of-factly.

Mitchell tapped his fingers on the rim of his hat, gathering his thoughts, no doubt coming up with another approach. "How would you arrange that?" he asked.

"How do you mean?"

"At the hotel?"

I shook my head. "On the ship."

"On the ship," he repeated to himself, staring at his drink. He hadn't touched it since his first sip. I wasn't sure if it was deliberate, his way of insinuating that he didn't need to drink his way through a crisis like I seemed to be doing. "You'd plan to tell them?"

"I don't know."

"The ship is sailing tonight."

"I know."

Mitchell decided we'd spent enough time chatting man-to-man. He started talking down to me. "I'm afraid I have to say no, Jim. I'm sorry, but I have to be firm about this. I came here to break the news to the children and to escort them home. It wasn't easy for me to do that, but it's what I feel I have to do." As if he hadn't said enough, he added, "I think Kathleen would have wanted me to."

That was it. I'd heard enough and I was getting tired of the pretense. I told him, "Maybe she would have wanted *me* to. . . ."

Whatever else Mitchell might be, he's no fool. He could see that I'd thrown down my reserve, and he must have sensed what was on its way out of the floodgates now that I'd opened them. He lamely conceded, "I'm sure she would have wanted us both to."

"How the hell do you know?" I snapped angrily. I was out of control and I could barely get the words out through my rage. "I spent half my life with her. You knew her five years. Five years! We met when she was seventeen! So don't tell *me* what she would have wanted!"

He recoiled from the outburst, and for a fleet second I saw fear in his face. And hurt. I'd struck out as hard as I could, but it was an empty gesture, and I knew it, although too late to do anything about it. In exchange for a cheap blow beneath the belt I'd sacrificed my fragile grip on myself. The tears were coming again, much as I tried to stop them. Mitchell seized on the opportunity to step in and make another bid for control of the situation.

"The children need strength, Jim," he told me with soft certainty.

I nodded, closing my eyes and taking a deep breath. You're blowing it, Tannen. Snap out of it. I tamed the trembling in my voice and went back to my original position. "I want this night with them."

"I don't think you're up to it," Mitchell countered.

"I'll be fine," I assured him, even though I was having my doubts. I had to make him understand. I wanted this settled without things getting any uglier. "I want to be with them," I explained. "Alone. Maybe more than just tonight. Maybe a couple of nights, I don't know."

"Is it two nights now, or what?" Mitchell said dryly. He was disgusted now.

"Until I'm ready!" I said it like a declaration of war. The other people on the patio were looking at us tentatively. They were all Greek, probably getting a real thrill seeing the Americans go at it. Maybe they'd come over and offer a few pointers if it dragged on any longer. The waiter took advantage of the lull in the action to flit by and drop off our check. We both ignored it. We had other things on our minds.

"Well," Mitchell said dourly, having had time to assess the situation and formulate a new strategy. "I'm not going to subject the children to a drama between you and me. They have enough grief in store. If you need more time with them, I'll respect that. . . . If you feel you must tell them yourself, well, I'll honor that, too."

He stood up. I stayed put.

"Your next stop is Cairo," he went on. "I'll be there at the Hilton. If I don't hear from you, I'll move on to the stop after that. Tunis. That's three days from now.

That ought to be time enough. I'll be waiting at the docks to take them home."

He leaned over the table and turned up the check long enough to see what it ran to, then went to his wallet.

"I'll get it," I told him.

"I've got it," he insisted, pulling out a few bills.

"I'll *get* it," I seethed, feeling a desperate futility.

He set the bills on the tray next to the check. "It's done," he informed me, then took up his hat and left.

I finished my drink, then stared at his, left barely touched. Damn him. Why did I have to hate myself for hating him?

I finished his drink, too.

CHAPTER TWENTY-TWO

There have been occasions in the past when I would awake to the dark of my unlit room hours before dawn, suddenly wide awake and held in the grips of an inexplicable but all-absorbing fear, triggered by no cause that could come to mind. It was always accompanied by a near paralysis and overwhelming sense of insignificance, as if my small, single bed had suddenly become an entire, empty world upon which I lay at the naked mercy of some distant, unfeeling force. It's hard to explain the raw vulnerability of those moments, but it would seem as if the universe were held together by mere whims and that at any second all the things I'd ever taken for granted would be suddenly snatched from me. I would dread the sudden scream of an ambulance, cringe at anticipated tremors that would crumble the house on top of me, hear outside my window the stealthy approach of those who had come to slay me for pleasure. It had always been the night that bred these terrors, and if the feelings didn't pass with the same fleeting speed by which they had come, they would always take their leave with the coming of dawn, like vampires whose only fear was the light of day.

But today it was different. The afternoon sun was

dodging clouds and burning down brightly on the city streets of Athens, and the sounds of mid-day activity were flourished by cheerful music drifting out from market squares; the sound of singing vendors and playing children. It was a day for the living, boasting promise and good cheer. Street performers swallowed swords or snapped fingers at trained dogs dancing in circles on their hind legs, while onlookers watched on and tossed a few drachmas onto the time-worn pavement. In the midst of all this spirited bustle, I walked in a state of numbed fear, my raw eyes hidden behind sunglasses that failed to make the world seem dark enough to match my mood. I was surrounded by thousands of people but I felt as alone and desolate as I had the previous night on the upper deck of the cruise ship.

I didn't want to run into the children, so whenever I surfaced from the depths of my melancholy and noticed that I was venturing near a part of the city that was crowded with tourists, I would cut back along the side streets and back alleys, passing heaps of litter, stray dogs, hard-eyed urchins and dozing beggars. The smells of rich Greek food wafted out from kitchens, mingling with the stench of refuse.

In Greece, as in Italy and other countries in Europe, midafternoon was a time for siesta, and I reached a residential section of town just as shops were closing for the next few hours and workers were drifting home. I was hungry and bought a sampling of figs and dates from a vendor just before he was about to pull the shade down over his cart. When I asked the price and paid what he asked without bartering, he seemed taken aback, as if I'd deprived him of the pleasure of his trade.

I sat down in a small nearby park to eat. It was a children's park, featuring a miniature bumper car ride and a row of three cartoonish animals resting on stands like the mechanical rocking horses you feed nickels to outside of supermarkets back in the states. Two young girls, both younger than Truman-Paul by several years,

were sitting on the rides, which weren't working. They
compensated by rocking back and forth in their seats
and squealing with delight. Soon their mother, a prema-
turely aged woman in black, came over and put coins
into the rides. The older girl jiggled atop a bouncing
camel while her sister held the reins of a dolphin that jolted
lightly back and forth. The rides lasted only a minute or
so, after which the children squirmed down and climbed
up onto the bumper car platform, picking out the cars
of their choice as they cried out to their mother. She, in
turn, moved toward a shed the size of a small kiosk set
alongside the ride. Presently, the door to the shed
opened and a man in coveralls emerged, his thick eyebrows arched in a look of irritation as he traded a few
words with the woman and took the coins she handed
him. He went to a control box and activated the cars,
then pulled a cigar from his pocket and bit off one end,
spitting it out angrily before lighting up and pacing
back and forth before the shed. There was a rustling in
the bushes behind the ride, and suddenly two young
boys were wriggling their way between the bars of the
ride's railing. They quickly ran over to two of the
sleeker-looking cars and hopped in behind the wheel.
This must have been the way Greeks learned to drive,
because the boys battered their cars around the track
with the same psychotic glee required to navigate the
streets of Athens. The attendant blew smoke and howled
at the boys, waving his fist threateningly. The boys
would ease off on their collision courses until the man
turned his back, then resume their mock demolition
derby, always looking to the older of the girls as if they
were vying for her favor like bucking rams in mating
season.

I watched all this as if through a fog. There was a
dreamlike unreality to the moment, an aura of sadness
hanging in the air that seemed comforting. There were
pigeons waddling in circles on the pavement in front of
me, and I flicked date pits at them, watching them fly

off, only to light on the ground a few yards away and wobble their way back.

Another man entered the park. Standing between myself and the bumper cars, he poked at his teeth with a toothpick as he watched the children. One of the boys slammed into the side of the car being ridden by the younger of the girls, and she started to cry. The attendant threw down his cigar and started up the steps leading to the track.

Both boys instantly bolted from their cars and bounded over the railing on the other side of the ride, vanishing into the bushes from which they had first appeared. The mother came over and picked up the youngest girl, rocking her in her arms until she stopped crying. When the mother looked to face the man with the toothpick, he quickly glanced away. I could see his features then, etched with despair and frustration. He was my age, but his hair was receding and streaked with grey, half-hidden beneath a small cap. I assumed that he and the woman were man and wife, caught up in their own melodrama.

Maybe he'd had an affair and she'd found out about it and was now relishing his display of anguished contrition. It was clear that he was burdened by some deep and troubling emotion, while her features were hardened. She sat down with the one daughter in her lap, while the other girl knelt on the seat beside her, peering over her mother's shoulders at the man, who offered a pained smile. When the girl smiled back, the mother sensed it and jerked her by the hem of the skirt to make her sit down so she couldn't see her father. The man's smile faded. He traded the toothpick for a cigarette, lit it, then stood with his hands in the pockets of his ragged coat, watching the others through the smoke, his face a cipher.

I was overcome by a desire to interrupt their bleak ritual, to tell them that there was nothing that could have happened between them to merit what they were doing to each other and their children. I wanted to make them see what they had, the joys they could be sharing, the opportunities that lay before them if they would only put aside their stubborness and selfishness. Look at me, I wanted to scream out to them. This is what becomes of those who take the course you're on. Don't do it to yourselves.

I said nothing, though. I crumpled the wrapper I'd bought my fruit in and pitched it in a trashcan, then left them. I started back toward the city and the port. There were more clouds overhead now, casting shadows on the pavement and sides of stone buildings. It was still siesta time, and it wasn't until I was back in the heart of the city that I found myself in the steady stream of pedestrians and traffic.

I was passing through a courtyard that was busy with activity when I heard a woman call out my name. I had been thinking about Kathleen and the voice shocked me. I looked around, uncomprehending, doubting my senses.

I saw a waving hand amidst the crowded tables of an outdoor cafe, then recognized Marie, smiling brightly at me as she got up from her chair. I stayed where I was, watching her come toward me, unable to move.

"Jim, what a surprise! It was raining in Naples, so we ended up driving straight through and taking a ferry from Reggio. We just got here an hour ago and. . . ." She stopped before me and stared at me with a look of horror as I removed my sunglasses. "Oh, my God, Jim. . . ."

"My wife," I croaked hoarsely. "She died. Kathleen's dead. . . ."

She took a step forward and put her arms around me. I clung to her, burying my face in her shoulder and letting my grief pour out over her. She stroked my hair and led me off to one side until I could regain my composure enough to let her know what had happened.

"I'm sorry," she whispered, her own eyes welling with tears. "I'm so sorry. . . ."

There was little more to be said. She stayed with me there in the courtyard a while longer, then, when I felt up to it, I said I wanted to walk some more.

"Do you want to be by yourself?" she asked.

I shook my head. "Come with me. Please."

"Of course."

She went back to her table long enough to pick up her purse and tell the rest of her group that she'd meet them back on the ship later, then we walked together through the maze of streets leading to the Acropolis. Neither of us said a word the whole time. She held my hand and occasionally glanced up at me. I figured that Mandy had probably already taken the children up to the ruins, so we went there, wandering amidst the glorious rubble and blocks of aged marble until we found a spot near the Erechtheum where we could be alone. I was feeling somewhat better now, the best I'd felt since hearing the news. I was ready to talk about it. She was ready to listen.

"You know, I never really believed we were finished. In a way, that's the hardest part to accept; that it's over for good." I took a deep breath and stared down at the city below. Kathleen and I had walked those streets once before, but we never would again. I told Marie, "I always thought there'd be another round; that I'd get another chance and the next time I wouldn't blow it. I'd be the world's greatest husband. The best lover. The best provider . . . the best father."

"You can still be the best father," she told me calmly.

I shook my head, running my hand along the weathered surface of a stone block beside me. "Marie, I'm a father like your ex-husband's a father."

She tilted her head to one side, confused. I went down a set of broken steps and started pacing in a clearing. "Phone calls on birthdays . . . I even forgot one of those, once . . . occasional weekends when I come to town . . . you know the type?" She kept watching me, but said nothing. "Marie, this is the first time I've spent more than five days with them in over four years. And you know what? I spent a lot of that time counting the days until it's over. The world's best father? I'm a disaster. Always have been. Always was."

I looked at Marie and smirked cynically. "You thought I was a good father."

"I still do, James."

"What? I don't understand how you can—"

"Your children adore you," she said to me. "And you them. It's obvious. It's all over your faces. You should see them light up when you come near."

I was exasperated. "Marie, youre just trying to be nice and I appreciate it, but you've got it wrong."

She came down the steps to join me. "You think you're like my ex-husband? Not at all."

"You haven't seen the way we fight," I argued.

"Yes I have, remember? God, what I'd give to see my girls fight with their father. Do you know how they fight? They sit like statues. Very polite. No one talks. *That's* a man who doesn't know how to be a father."

I couldn't believe what I was hearing. I watched her come toward me in the ruins. Was she a Muse or a Siren trying to lure me to doom with her assurances? She stopped before me, looking up, studying my ravaged face so closely I felt shame.

"You'll do fine with them. You'll do well." She put a hand to my face, as if to further assure me. Then she pulled it back and probed my eyes with hers. "Anyway, you don't have a choice, do you? They're your children, and they belong to you. They're yours now. Forever."

CHAPTER TWENTY-THREE

Dusk was bathing the Acropolis in a golden hue as I boarded the ship with Marie. We walked together as far as her room, then paused outside her door.

"I want to thank you for all your help, Marie," I told her. "You've made a big difference."

"I'm glad I could do something," she said, opening her door. "Would you like to come in?"

I smiled and shook my head. "Thanks, but I want to track down the children."

"Good luck with them." She leaned up and kissed me lightly on the cheek. "You'll do fine, trust me."

"I'll let you know how it goes."

"Good."

I hurried back to my cabin, resolved to hold myself together. Mitchell had been right about one thing. They needed strength. He might have been right about a lot of other things, too, but I wasn't prepared to deal with those. Not just yet.

To my surprise, the children weren't back yet. I washed up quickly, then left a note for them to join me in the dining room. I wasn't hungry, but all I'd had to eat all day was the handful of dates and figs, so I figured I should have something.

I reached the dining room just as Mr. Peachum, the old widower, was finishing his meal. I came over to his table.

"Mr. Peachum?"

He looked up, slightly startled. "Uh, yes?" I could see he didn't recognize me.

"I'm James Tannen. You met my daughter a few nights back and—"

"Ah, yes!" he said, nodding to himself. "A nice young woman."

"She sure is."

"What's that?" I'd moved around to the other side of the table. He turned his head accordingly and I guessed he was deaf in his left ear. I moved back to his right side.

"Can I sit down a moment?"

"Yes, yes, of course," he said, delighted. A waiter swooped over and set a cup of tea in front of Mr. Peachum, then asked if I wanted a drink. I started to order a brandy, but changed my mind.

"I'll have coffee, please."

Mr. Peachum leaned to one side and squinted toward our table. "I don't see your youngsters."

"They took a tour with the activities director," I told him as the waiter brought my coffee.

"I have three grandchildren," the old man said. "A little older than yours, but not much."

"Mr. Peachum, I wanted to apologize for the other night. I was having a few problems with my oldest, and—"

He waved a hand over his tea. "Not to worry."

"I was wondering if you'd like to join us tonight. I know you've just eaten, but you can just come over to talk and listen. We'd be glad to have your company."

"Thanks, kind of you to offer," he said, stirring cream into his tea. "But after I eat I like to go to the ship's chapel." He paused a moment to add a packet of imitation sugar to his drink. Then he resumed his stirring, watching the swirl of cream and granules mix with the tea. His voice became a little raspy when he spoke again, not looking up from his cup. "You see, my wife died just before the cruise. She always wanted to tour the Mediterranean, but we kept putting it off until our children booked us on this tour for our anniversary. Fifty years we were married, Sylvia and I. Fifty wonderful years. I go to the chapel after dinner every night and tell her all the things I've seen during the day. I like to think she can hear me, somehow." He set his spoon down a took a sip from the tea, then continued, "I think she would have wanted me to go on this trip. So much of her is a part of me, I feel sometimes like she's actually here. Today, when we came off the boat and I first saw the Acropolis, I even turned to point it out to her. It was something you'd expect from a foolish old man, don't you think?"

"No," I said hoarsely. "No, sir, I don't think that at all."

He sipped his tea once more, then pulled an antique stopwatch from his vest pocket and checked the time. "Well, I really must be going. And I thank you for your offer. Perhaps I can join you another time?"

"Of course," I told him, offering a hand. "A pleasure to meet you, sir."

"And you," he said, getting up. "Give my best wishes to your children. They seem a lovely bunch."

"They are, sir. The best."

I watched Mr. Peachum slowly leave the dining room, glad that I'd taken the time to talk to him. I wondered if I'd have been able to bear up as well as he seemed to be under his circumstances. He, and Marie for that matter, seemed to possess a quiet strength and basic integrity I found lacking in myself. Measured against them, I felt a lot like a spoiled, whining child hell-bent on wailing with self-pity over my misfortunes. I was acting in character, after all. James the Jerk. Your bed's been made, Tannen. Sleep in it.

"Hey, J.P.!" Truman-Paul yipped, rushing up to the table, waving something in his small hand. Tilde and Trung were following close behind.

"Whoah, whoah!" I said, reaching out to hold Truman-Paul back from colliding into the table. "What do you have there, partner, huh?"

It was an old battered ring with worn images on its surface. It looked like it was made with tin and came out of a gumball machine years ago. Truman-Paul excited exclaimed, "We found it in the ruins! Isn't it great? I bet it's a thousand years old!"

"It's a real find, all right," I told him. "So you had a good time, then?"

"Hi, Dad," Tilde said, taking a good look at me. "How are you feeling?"

"Much better, thanks. Sit down, sit down. I bet you guys are starved."

"Put it on!" Truman-Paul said, grabbing for my fingers with the ring. Besides being bent, it was too small for my hand. Truman-Paul was disappointed.

"Hold it, hold it," I told him, reaching behind my neck and unfastening my gold chain long enough to slip the ring onto it so that it dangled in plain view with my collar open. "There, ready to ward off evil and give me magic powers, right?"

"Right!" Truman bubbled, sitting down.

"I'm sure glad you're better," Trung told me as he picked up his menu. "That woman who took us around was crazy."

"She was *not*," Tilde said.

Truman-Paul curled his fingers on top of his head to imitate Mandy's hairstyle, then started doing an impersonation of her. " 'Ooooooh, here's where they took their 'neat' baths, and here's where they made their 'neat' laws. . . .'"

Trung joined in on the roast. " 'And they built all these 'far out' temples for Athena. Isn't that 'neat'? They worshipped a *woman*!' "

"Stop it, you two!" Tilde said angrily. "You're horrible!"

"Oh, come on, Tilde," Truman-Paul said, "She was so dumb. . . ."

"She was very nice, and trying very hard," Tilde said. "She's just in the wrong job."

Trung complained, "Aw, you feel sorry for everybody. . . ."

I had trouble keeping a straight face, watching them go at it, obviously enjoying every minute. Even Tilde finally ended up joining the bandwagon and making fun of Mandy. They talked nonstop all through dinner, barely giving me a chance to put in a word edgewise. I was content to just watch them and marvel at their presence. Thinking of what Mr. Peachum had said about his wife, I glanced occasionally over at the empty chair at our table, trying to picture Kathleen there, sharing the moment with us. Look at them, Kathy. Aren't they wonderful? If we're responsible for them, then we must have done something right, don't you think? Kathy?

"Hey, Dad, are you okay?" Truman-Paul asked.

I smiled down at him. "Yeah, I'm fine, Truman. I'm doing just fine."

I wanted to spend more time with them after supper, so I managed to get them dressed up enough to go to the grand ballroom, where the band was playing a night of oldies for the non-disco crowd. I even let Trung have a glass of spiked punch. One glass. Most of the music was even before my time, although it brought back memories of childhood nights in the family room of my first home in North Kingstown, Rhode Island, where my parents spent winter nights playing records on the Victrola while they watched a fire blaze in the hearth. That seemed like a long, long time ago.

I was surprised to see Mr. Peachum there, wearing a dark suit and swaying his head in time with the music, caught up in his own memories, pleasant ones from the expression on his face. When the song ended and promptly sequed into another, he adjusted his tie and walked across the room to where a group of three older women sat at a table, staring out at the proceedings. He asked one of them to dance, and after making her night by whisking her gently around the room, he returned her to the table and repeated the same performance with the other two women. Our eyes met at one point and he winked happily. I'm sure Sylvia was proud of him.

The band wrapped up its medley, then made an announcement about a late night buffet being held at the grill before starting in on another tune. I looked over at Tilde. She was smiling as she watched Mr. Peachum. She'd put a ribbon in her hair and used a little make-up on her face. Over twenty years ago I'd fallen in love with a girl that looked just like her. It almost broke my heart just to look at her, the resemblance was so uncanny. As it was, though, I moved over to her and bowed slightly.

"May I have this dance?"

"Oh, Daddy. . . ." she laughed. When I started to guide her to the dance floor, though, she started to protest. "No, Daddy, I don't want to . . . I don't know how."

I put an arm around her and held her other hand up, then slowly led, looking down on her lovingly. She moved stiffly at first, but followed my lead instinctively. When she stopped looking at her feet and glanced up at me, I said, "Who says you can't? Look at you. You're great!"

She blushed a little and it made her look even more radiant. We moved around the dance floor and her confidence increased. I spotted Trung and Truman-Paul watching us approvingly. All seemed right with the world. If only. . . .

I looked back down at Tilde. When I dipped her slightly she tossed her head in a way Kathleen used to when we danced. I swallowed hard, smiling with pride.

"You're going to be a beautiful lady, Matilda."

She smiled back at me. "If I can look half as nice as Mom I'll be happy."

It was the band's last number, and when they finished it and went on break, the children admitted they were tired. We went back to our cabins and I saw them off to bed. As I was tucking Truman-Paul in, he asked me, "Are you going to be well enough to go with us tomorrow?"

"I'm not sure yet," I told him.

"Wear the ring all night and see what happens," he advised me.

"You bet I will." I kissed him and Tilde, then went down the hallway to the deck. I wasn't tired. We were passing by the island of Crete. By morning we would be in Cairo, where Mitchell would be waiting. I wasn't sure what to do about it. I spent close to an hour going back and forth in my mind, trying to make the right decision. I came up with a lot more questions than answers.

Two minutes later I was knocking on the door to Marie's cabin. There was no answer at first, but just before I knocked again she opened the door, toweling off her wet hair. She was wearing only a bathrobe. I nodded a greeting and strode past her, caught up in my thoughts.

"You once told me that your kids drove you crazy, that your friends made you go on this cruise because they thought you were going to lose your mind. Did you say that?"

"Yes," she said, watching me pace around her cabin.

"Are you busy?" I said, almost as an afterthought.

"No." She had an intrigued smile on her face.

I rattled on, "You said that being alone with them was too much for you. You said that, right? That you didn't have time to do anything? Or see anyone? That they just 'overwhelmed' you? Wasn't that the word you used? 'Overwhelmed'?"

She nodded, still dabbing at her hair with the towel.

She seemed puzzled now, and I couldn't blame her. I hardly knew what I was getting at myself. I was just trying to throw everything out where we could take a good look at it.

"What if there was someone who your kids really liked? I mean *really* liked. Loved, even. Someone who was wonderful with them . . . and *wouldn't* be driven crazy by them. Wouldn't even be overwhelmed, and you knew in your heart that you *would* be overwhelmed . . . and you weren't sure if you'd be any good for them at all, and you didn't know what was the right thing to do, or the wrong thing to do, and you were scared, and confused, and there was this 'person'. . . ." My voice was starting to tremble. God help me, I was seeing it from Mitchell's side. ". . . and all he wanted was to be good for them. I mean, you could still see your kids whenever you wanted, no problem. It wouldn't be like they'd be taken away from you . . . because all he wanted was . . . was just to take care of them. . . ."

I paused to gather my breath, wondering if I was making any sense. I looked at Marie.

She had lowered the towel and was staring at me firmly, with no trace of a smile anymore. "I would fight him to the death," she whispered forcefully.

"Right!" I said, feeling a surge of relief. I headed back for the door. "Thanks," I told her. "What are you doing tomorrow?"

She gestured with open palms that she had no plans.

"I'll call you." I kissed her quickly on my way out the door. "You're wonderful."

I went straight to my cabin and forced myself to lie down and sleep. I wanted all my strength for the next day.

CHAPTER TWENTY-FOUR

The docks outside Cairo were snarled with the usual mass of frenzied humanity—tour-guides, souvenir salesmen, beggars, and street performers, all crowding around the platforms leading down from ships moored in the harbor. We'd been there for more than an hour, so the exodus from the ship had dwindled down to a trickle by the time I came down the ramp, keeping an eye open for Mitchell. I finally spotted him, waiting patiently in the area roped off for disembarking passengers. When he saw me, his eyes instinctively moved past me for a look at the children. He didn't see them.

"Where are they?" he asked when I caught up to him.

"They're not here," I told him. Marie had taken them ashore earlier. By now they were probably riding camels somewhere in the desert. I'd told the kids I'd come down sick again during the night and was going to have to see another doctor in the city."

"Your message said—"

"—that I wanted to see you."

He was clearly upset. "There's a plane for New York at twelve o'clock."

"We're not ready to go to New York," I said. "I want to talk to you." Without waiting for his response, I walked on down to the end of the blocked-off area, then paused until he could catch up with me.

I was glad for all the pandemonium around us as we sought out a place we could talk. I was still putting my thoughts together, trying to prepare myself for what I knew was in store for both of us. Mitchell was quiet, too, probably in the same frame of mind. I wasn't looking forward to this.

We settled on an indoor cafe in the old part of town. It looked like a set out of *Casablanca*, complete with slow-whirring ceiling fans chasing hot air and stray flies around the room, pushing both downward at us. We both ordered bottled beers. I was determined to match him sip for sip, and if he was going to just stare at his drink, I was ready to do the same. The heat was almost oppressive, and sweat beaded up on both of our brows as we faced off on either side of a wood table just inside the entrance.

Mitchell poured out half a glass of beer and promptly drank it down, then wiped his lips with the back of his hand before going to his pocket for a handkerchief he could use to wipe his face. "Let's have it," he said impatiently.

I filled my glass and held onto it, tilting it so foam rolled around the inside rim. The coolness felt good on my fingers. I chose my words carefully. "I just realized that everything was happening a little too fast for me . . . that I hadn't had time to really think things through. If you know what I mean."

He didn't say anything. He snapped away a fly in a way that suggested he was prepared to do the same with anything I had to say.

I said it anyway. "Things feel different now. Kathleen kind of held everything together. . . . Now there's just you . . . and there's me . . . and there's the children." I took a drink, waiting for him to respond. He just stared at me. Now I knew how I must have looked to him just before my outburst the day before. "Do you understand what I'm saying, Mitchell?"

He sighed as if he was bored by my indirectness. Shifting in his seat, he blandly asked, "You're suggesting some kind of alteration in the present custody arrangement?" It was Mitchell Arnaud, Attorney-at-Law, speaking, loud and clear.

"I'm just exploring," I said, cursing myself at the same time for letting myself be intimidated. "I'd like to know how you feel about it."

"Well, let me tell you then," he said glibly. "I won't allow it. I simply won't do it. I won't agree." I could see he was only warming up. He was in his element now. "Oh, you could go to court and fight me for them, but you'd ruin everyone in the process, and, quite frankly, you wouldn't stand a chance."

"Why do you say that?" I muttered, reeling inside. I'd come into this with the foolish hope that we might be able to reason it all out, but he'd jumped to the offensive and seemed determined to keep the conversation on that level.

"Because I know the law," he said curtly.

"But I'm their father."

"Matter of definition."

"And biology," I rallied.

Mitchell scoffed, "Truman-Paul has a fishtank full of guppies. They have babies, too, but I wouldn't call those 'fathers' swimming around in there. Trung's in a different category, but what he needs is a strong disciplinary hand and the example of a man who works hard and commands respect in this world. He's prone to take the easy way, you know."

"If that's supposed to be a slap at me, Mitchell. . . ."

"How could you support them?" he went on as if I hadn't spoken. "Let's get down to it. That's what counts in a court of law, especially after a father's abandoned ship." I opened my mouth to speak, but he was ahead of me again. "And don't tell me about your two hundred thousand dollar escrow. I've checked you out, and you owe more than that to the Franklin Savings Bank."

In professional boxing, there are times when one of the fighters takes a particular blow to the face or body and suddenly is out of the match. He might continue to stand, or even hold his fists up before him, but it's clear to anyone watching that the fight's been knocked out of him and he's nothing but fair game if the referee doesn't step in. I was outmatched by Mitchell, but there was no one there to intervene for me. I just sat there and took it, buying time, hoping I could summon back the nerve that had abandoned me somewhere between here and the docks.

"We're talking about tutors and teachers, and ballet classes and housekeepers and babysitters and team uniforms and orthodontists and special schools . . . Truman-Paul has a learning disability. . . ."

"I know that," I said feebly.

"I'm surprised you do," he answered coldly.

"I've been working with him."

"I'm not impressed," Mitchell snapped. He was through pulling punches. Raising his voice to match his temper, he seethed, "Where were you when his learning disability *started*? When he needed your reassurance and support? Where were you when he wished more than anything that you could see him in his school play? Or when Tilde prayed you'd surprise her by showing up for her recital, or Trung to one of his soccer games?"

He was rattling them off like a list of crimes, which they were. I was guilty on all counts and I knew it. Swept up with his surge of emotion, Mitchell's voice was like a shout being held back by only the thinnest leash, a leash that was breaking, strand by strand, as he spoke.

"Where were you when it was time for having tonsils out, when Tilde cried so piteously they had to put her in a soundproof room? Do you know about any of that?

When she came out of the anesthesisa, she wept over *you*!"

He was almost out of his seat in his rage, leaning across the table, daring me to avoid his livid gaze.

"And where were you . . . Goddamn you, son-of-a-bitch, when I held them in my arms and reassured them that you still loved them, even, when on their birthdays, you were nowhere to be found."

"One time. . . ." I whispered.

"Where were you?" he shouted, drowning me out. "Where were you?!!!" His hands were shaking, as if he wanted to grab me with them. "WHERE WERE YOU?!!!"

I didn't have to answer that. We both knew where I'd been. I could feel the eyes of everyone in the cafe staring at me, like a jury that wouldn't be wasting much time coming to a verdict about my guilt. Mitchell sat back, judging the effect of his accusation. He guessed my thoughts and told me, "I'm a damn good lawyer, fella. If I had to, I could make Mother Theresa look unfit to run an orphanage without telling a single lie. You, you're a piece of cake."

And so, there it was. We were both silent. The fans spun quietly overhead. Flies buzzed around the table. Customers and cafe workers murmured to one another. Outside, life went on in the streets as if we didn't exist.

Then I spoke, resting my case. "I love them, Mitchell."

He looked at me with disgust. "You don't even know them."

"That's not true."

He raised his eyebrows mockingly. "What are their friends' names? Who are their teachers? What do they dream about at night? Where do you touch each one of them to make them giggle? Which one's had chicken pox? Which one has—"

"I'm talking about the future."

"So am I!" Mitchell retorted. "I've put a lot into those children and I'm prepared to put in a lot more. Their college educations are secured and in the bank, and I'll make any other arrangements I have to to see that their needs are tended to. I'm not going to back down on this."

I thought he was through with me, but he reached into his suitcase pocket as he stood up and withdrew an envelope. "I thought I might be able to spare you this," he said, "but it should clear up any doubts you might have . . . at least about what Kathleen would have wanted. I think we'll both agree she would have known best."

He put the envelope down the the table in front of me. All the pent-up anger had been released, and now he was reduced to the verge of tears. "You see, I love them, too," he said thickly. "More than you'll ever know. Or understand." He started off, then stopped and looked back at me. "I won't follow you around anymore. The trip ends in Genoa. That's where I'll be waiting."

I stayed where I was a long time after he had left, going over the confrontation again and again, feeling lower each time I heard him recounting my failures as a parent, as a human being. There had been times the past few days when I thought I'd been too hard on myself, but I realized now that I'd actually been too lenient.

I paid the bill and took the envelope outside. It had Mitchell's name on the front and I recognized the handwriting as Kathleen's. I knew how Pandora felt the day she opened the box. There was a mosque across the street, and as I walked in the shade of its solemn portico, hearing even more solemn chants sounding from within, I pried open the envelope and withdrew a single sheet of paper. It was dated several months ago, but it read like a message delivered from a fresh grave half a world away.

Mitchell—

On this milestone of a birthday (forty seems like the most dramatic passage of all, at least today), I have been reflecting on my own mortality and counting all the things for which I am grateful. Mostly, Mitchell, it is for you, and the gift you've given me, and the children, of knowing a man whose arms and heart are big enough to shelter us all, and who manages the world with the same honesty and gentle authority that he manages the tantrum of a child. I thank you for rescuing us, and for sustaining us . . . for giving me the peace of mind of knowing that, at last, my children have a father.

—Your devoted Kathleen.

I wandered from the mosque in a daze. Near the edge of the nearest market square there was a well, long dried-up and now filled with refuse. I'd never before so much as considered suicide, but as I crumpled up the letter and tossed it down the black maw of the well, I couldn't help but think it might be best for all concerned if I could be rid of myself as easily.

CHAPTER TWENTY-FIVE

I flagged down a cabby driving an open-topped white jeep and told him to take me to Ibrahim's Tomb in the City of the Dead, where I'd arranged to meet Marie and the children. They were sitting at an outdoor cafe sipping lemonades when I pulled up. Truman-Paul was the first to spot me and he bolted happily from his seat, almost upsetting the table.

"Hi, Dad!" he cried out, running over. "You should have seen us. We were riding *camels*!"

The others joined us. Tilde took a good look at me and said, "You don't look much better, Dad."

I was beyond the point of hiding it. "I'll manage," I said lamely, trying to avoid Marie's gaze. It was no use, though. As the children piled into the back seats, talking excitedly about our upcoming visit to the Great Pyramids, she came over to me.

"Jim. . . ."

"I don't want to talk about it," I whispered bitterly, refusing to look at her.

"Would you rather I didn't come?" she asked.

"No," I said. "Do . . . please."

She laid her hand gently on my forearm, just long enough for me to take notice, then she climbed in back

174

and started talking with the kids so they wouldn't bother me. She was better than I deserved. So were the kids. I knew I was going to have to tell them today.

We rode out of the city, catching a faint dose of the khamsin, a hot breath of wind that sweeps in from across the desert during spring and early summer, stirring up the sands of the Muqattam Hills that flank the pyramids. We all covered our eyes when the gust pushed a cloud of sand over the jeep. The driver fortunately was used to this and was wearing goggles, enabling him to forge ahead so that by the time the wind died down and we were able to venture a gaze at our surroundings, the Sphinx loomed before us like a collossus guard dog protecting the Pyramids. The children gasped with awe at the sight, and I was moved as well. As with most of the world's great wonders, seeing them in books or on postcards does little to prepare one for coming upon them in their full-scale glory.

Our driver pulled off the road and dropped us off, then we slowly walked up an inclined walkway to the stone frame of a doorway set amidst ruins overlooking the Sphinx. Moments passed as we took in the monuments, then Truman-Paul asked, "Why did they do these?"

He was looking up to me under the brim of his baseball cap, all childish innocence and wonder. I told him, "To try and make themselves permanent, Truman."

He looked back at the Sphinx, satisfied with my answer. "It worked."

"Did it?" I said sadly. "It's face is half-gone. One day there'll be nothing here except sand. These were just a man's dreams. That's all they were. A man's dreams won't keep him alive."

Marie must have sensed what was coming, because she slowly moved away from us to the other side of the ruins. The children had their eyes on me now. Even they had been able to pick up on my mood.

"Nothing's permanent," I told them, searching out the words. "Nothing stays the same. There's no way of knowing what's going to happen next. The only thing you can ever be sure of, is . . . that whatever you think is going to happen . . . probably won't."

I turned away from them and passed back through the stone doorway, my back to the Sphinx. They followed, keeping their distance. There was suspicion in Trung's and Tilde's eyes. Truman-Paul was only confused at this stage.

"I didn't know that . . . when I was your age. I thought . . . I thought that everything would always work out the way I wanted it to." I was having trouble talking. I looked up, gathering my breath, trying to force back the tears and summon forth some strength. I was able to go on, but my voice was raspy and clogged with trapped emotion. "Like my marriage to your Mom, for instance. I thought it was a permanent thing. I really thought . . . we had something . . . something as permanent and lasting as these pyramids. . . . Or maybe more. But it wasn't. I lost her . . . because . . . those things happen. She couldn't be in my life any longer, not the way I wished she were . . . but life went on. It wasn't too easy . . . but it went on. As it always must. No matter what."

The wind picked up again, driving a funnel of raised sand across the ruins around us. I took advantage of the distraction to wipe at my eyes. I looked over at Marie, who was watching me with concern. Strength, Marie, I called out to her in my mind. Give me the strength to see this through. But there was nothing she could do now. It was all up to me. I went on, my voice wavering.

"The wonderful thing . . . about having you children . . . is that . . . your mother and I . . . and the proof of our love for each other . . . live on. Because part of each of us is alive . . . in you . . . I can see Kathleen in your eyes—looking out at me . . . and hear her . . . in your voices. So, you see . . . she's always around. No matter where she is. No matter where."

There was fear in the children's eyes now. Fear, terror, looks of confusion on the threshold of disbelief.

"I didn't plan . . . to talk about this right now. But I can't keep it to myself any longer." Tears were rolling hotly down my cheeks now, gathering up the fine dust of blown sand. I forced myself to look at them. "It's the most awful thing you'll ever hear."

Tilde instinctively took a step towards Truman-Paul. Trung crossed his arms, bracing himself.

"Your Mom . . . whom I dearly loved. And who you all dearly loved . . . has had to leave all of our lives now.

"Last week . . . she was taking the dog to the vet. There was a rainstorm . . . and the car . . . went out of control. Something happened."

"No. . . ." Truman-Paul whimpered.

"She was killed."

They were stunned, immobile. One by one, they began to weep.

"She was killed instantly," I said, drained. "There was no pain."

"Nooo!" Truman-Paul screamed, thrusting his face against his sister's chest. Tilde put her arms around him and held him close. Tears poured down her cheeks as she stared at me bravely. "He'll be fine," she assured me with a whisper. "I'm okay." She bit her lip, then repeated, "I'm okay."

I crouched down and hugged them both. There was nothing more for me to say. I looked over my shoulder and saw that Trung had walked back through the doorway and was standing with his back turned to us, staring downward. I came over to him. When I put a hand on his shoulder, he jerked it away, sobbing. I took him by both shoulders and turned him around to face me, then embraced him tightly as I led him back to be with the others. We all huddled together for some time. Marie had moved further off, wanting us to be alone.

Tilde finally spoke as she wiped at her tears. "Does Mitchell know?"

"Yes, he does," I said, acknowledging my final defeat. "He'll be waiting in Genoa . . . to take you home."

CHAPTER TWENTY-SIX

The ship had navigated back out into the Mediterranean by sunset, which came with the dark clouds of another coming storm. None of us were hungry, so we skipped dinner and gathered together in my cabin, where we stayed for several hours, listening to the storm break outside. There were deep bellows of thunder and jagged prongs of lightning stirring up the sea like pitchforks. Word came over the intercom that if the storm persisted, our progress would be slowed considerably and we might not reach Tunis until late the following night. The children, already wracked with grief, now were overcome by fear as well.

"We aren't going to sink, are we, Dad?" Truman-Paul asked, huddling close to me. We were sitting on my bed, except for Trung, who was curled up in one of the chairs.

"I don't think so, Tru," I told him. "I think this storm just looks and sounds worse than it actually is."

"I wonder how bad it was raining when Mom died."

"I don't know, Truman-Paul."

Tilde remembered. "It was raining the night we tried to call her. Was that the night she died?"

"I don't know, Tilde." I shivered inside as I thought

back to that night and recalled that I was with Marie. Not that night, I hoped.

Another flash of lightning brightened our cabin a moment, and I saw Trung pulled up into a ball, his face hidden behind the arms folded across his knees. I was going to tell him to come over and join us, but decided against it. We'd all have to work it out in our own ways.

"Julius Cesar!" Truman-Paul suddenly blurted out. "Did anything happen to him?"

"Mitchell said he'll be fine. He had some cuts on his paws and tail, but nothing serious."

"That's good," he said, settling back down. "He's a good dog."

"Who cares about the dog!" Trung yelled, raising his head. He'd been crying. "Maybe if the dog died, then—"

"Trung!" I interrupted. "Come on, cool it."

"Maybe I don't want to 'cool it'!" There was menace in his voice and his dark, wet eyes glistened like hard stones. "Damn smelly old dog got to live and she had to die just because she was taking him to the vet for—"

"All right, Trung. That's enough! Don't make this any harder, okay?"

"It wasn't Julius Caesar's fault!" Truman-Paul said.

"How do you know?" Trung said. "Maybe he was jumping around in the seat or something and made her lose control. Did you think about that?"

"It doesn't matter now, Trung," Tilde said. "What's done is done."

Trung got up from his chair and headed for the door. "I'm going to bed."

"Trung, wait. . . ." I called out, but he was already gone.

"He can be so mean sometimes," Tilde said.

"He's just upset," I said. "We all are. Maybe it's best if we all got some sleep."

"I'm not tired," Truman-Paul said. "I can't sleep when it's storming."

"Dad's right, Truman," Tilde said, getting up from the bed. "Come on. I'll read to you."

Truman-Paul hesitated, then took Tilde's hand as she helped him up. I kissed them both. "Your Dad loves you a lot. Don't you ever forget that, okay? And no matter what happens, I'm going to do a better job of staying close to you, even if it can only be in my heart."

They returned my kisses. Truman-Paul said, "We love you, too."

I walked them to their room, then went over to check on Trung. When I knocked on his door, he didn't answer. The door was locked.

"Come on, Trung, let me in."

"Leave me alone," he called out. "I just want to be left alone."

"Trung. . . ."

"I mean it!"

I paused, not sure how to handle it. "Are you sure, Trung?"

"Let me be!" I could tell he was still crying.

"Okay, but I'll leave my door unlocked if you want to come talk. Good night, Trung."

He didn't answer me. Before I went back into my room, I stopped a moment outside the door to the other kids' room. I could hear Truman-Paul and Tilde talking.

"Do you think she knew it was coming?"

"I don't know, Truman-Paul."

They were both calm now. I could picture them, lying on their sides, facing one another, helping each other.

"I think the windshield wipers were bad," Truman-Paul said after a moment's silence.

"Don't think about it, Truman-Paul. It's not going to make her come back."

"I know. Tilde, do you think she had a good life?"

My eyes were misting just listening to them.

"Yes," Tilde answered.

"She laughed a lot," Truman-Paul said.

"She did."

"So, I bet she had a happy life."

"I think so, Truman-Paul."

"Tilde . . . ?"

"Yes?"

There was another pause, then Truman-Paul said, "Never mind. Goodnight."

"Goodnight."

"Tilde . . . Dad wasn't really sick, was he?"

"I don't think so, Truman-Paul. I think he found out about Mom that night he got called. He just didn't want to tell us until we were ready."

"He sure looked like he was sick, though."

"He loved Mom a lot, Truman-Paul. You'd have looked sick, too, if you were him."

"Do I look sick now?"

"No, you look tired. Let's go to sleep."

"Okay."

They both fell silent. I went into my room, hearing a dull rumble of thunder. The storm was moving away from us, I paced around the room, but I couldn't convince myself I was tired. There was some unfinished business still hanging over me, and I wanted to take care of it.

Marie wasn't in her room, but I found her in the dining room, having late dessert by herself. She looked up at me with a noncommittal stare as I sat down across from her.

"Hi," I said weakly.

She was eating and didn't say anything.

"I was hoping we could talk."

"I see." She dabbed her lips with the corner of her napkin. "What about?"

"You know as well as I do, Marie. I saw the look on your face when you heard the kids were going back with Mitchell."

"I was surprised, that's all."

"No you weren't. You knew it when I first pulled up in the jeep at the cafe."

"I don't see that it's all that important what I think—"

"Bullshit," I told her. "It makes a *lot* of difference to *me*. I want you to understand. You don't know the whole situation like I do. I'm doing the right thing in letting him take them. It's the most unselfish thing I've done in all my life, and I don't pretend to be happy about it, but, damn it, it's the right thing to do."

"Only you can be the judge of that, James," she said.

"Then why are you passing judgment on me for doing it? Why are you trying to make me feel guilty about it?"

She started to get up, but I grabbed her by the wrist and set her back down. She looked down coldly at my hand and said, "What are you doing?"

I pulled my hand away. "I'm sorry. But don't you see, Marie. I care about your opinion of me. *Mon ami*, remember? You're my friend."

She sighed, sitting back in her chair. The look on her face gradually softened. So did her voice. "Your decision frightens me, James. It tears at my heart."

"But I don't see why. . . ."

"It makes me want to hurry home to be with my children. Maybe I'll never leave them again. Maybe my husband wouldn't take mine, either, if something happened to me."

"Marie, it's not the same thing. Not at all. Look, Mitchell has been a father to them for the past five years. He's given them love and care and more than I could ever hope to. Do you have someone doing that for your children now?"

She shook her head, looking down at her empty plate.

"Then, you see, it's a completely different situation. Right? Tell me I'm right, Marie."

"Yes, James," she said with resignation. "You're right. My children have no man to watch over them, no one

they can look up to as a father. If I died, there would be
no one like this, this Mitchell." She looked up at me and
I could see she was crying. "Or like you."

I was stunned. She got up from her chair and strode
off, her head bowed.

"Marie, wait!"

I followed her outside the dining room. It was still
raining hard, and she stopped under the cover of the
stairway leading up to the next deck. I came over to
her.

"Marie, I'm confused," I told her. "The other night,
when we were together, you said that you—"

"I know what I said," she said, sniffing back tears. "I
said what you needed to hear, what I needed to hear so
that it would not hurt so much." I tried to touch her but
she shrank away, leaning against the wall behind her.
"Please go, James."

"No. Not until I can make some sense of all this."

She laughed piteously. "Is it that complicated, James?
I am a woman who has been alone for too long. I do not
want to be alone forever. I want a man to love, a man
who can make me feel whole and bring smiles to the
faces of my children. Do you really think I am here to
jump from bed to bed like some cheap whore on a
holiday?"

"I never thought that, Marie. You know it, too." I
moved closer to her. "Listen, I can see this is all my
fault, as usual. I had no idea that you . . . that you and
I . . . Jesus, why does everything I touch have to fall
apart in my hands?"

Lightning flashed across the sea, and a shift in the
winds blew rain in at us. I leaned back against the wall
next to Marie and we both looked out at the downpour,
giving ourselves a moment to think.

"Life can play strange games on a person, can't it?"
Marie said.

"Amen to that," I said.

She turned her head and whispered, "I'm sorry. It

was my fantasy. You can't blame yourself for not seeing it."

"You're a tremendous person," I told her. "If I were looking for someone, I couldn't think of a better person to fall in love with."

"Except for your wife."

I nodded. "Well, that's something I'll just have to work out. In the meantime, though, I'm still in the market for close friends. Think we can work something out?"

She smiled shyly. "I would like to try. Very much."

"Let's shake on it." I held a hand out to her. She took it eagerly, then pulled me forward enough to kiss me. It was short and tender. It felt right.

I walked her back to her room, with neither of us saying much. When we stopped before her door, I said, "You ever been to California?"

She shook her head.

"If you ever decide to, you've got a tour-guide. Mucho cheapo."

She laughed. The laughter of chimes. Who knows, another time and I really might have fallen for her.

"Good night, James."

"Good night, Marie."

As she was closing her door, she looked me in the eye and said, 'I still say the children would be happiest with you."

Her words followed me back to my room and climbed into bed with me. They wouldn't let me sleep.

CHAPTER TWENTY-SEVEN

The next day was well-suited for mourning. Although the full fury of the storm was long behind us, a steady drizzle fell for all but a few hours. We spent most of the time in our rooms, adjusting to the pervasive sadness that had overcome us all. I stayed with the children as much as I felt they wanted me to.

There were long periods of time when none of us spoke, but now and then we would strike up small conversations, if only to take our minds off the reality of Kathleen's death for a few minutes. It was a special, however tragic, time, giving us a chance to discuss a lot of the things that were seldom brought up when we were together in the past. Trivial insights, retellings of daily routines, half-thoughts and petty gripes—they all spilled out in quiet talk, like the idle chatter of old friends. I was thankful for the chance to be with them like this, although I cursed the fact that it had taken so crushing a blow to open us up. The grim beauty of it was that it all seemed to come out so naturally, not forced or pretentious.

Only Trung was holding back. He would be there, half-listening, occasionally putting in a few words, but his mind was far away, and whenever I tried to reach him he made it clear that he didn't want me prying. When the rain let up for a short time in the mid-afternoon, he went outside, and when we went to track him down on our way to supper, we found him sitting in one of the lifeboats, legs crossed, oblivious to everything. He didn't want to join us, and I had to hold myself back from insisting.

Mr. Peachum joined us for dinner that night. When he learned that the children had lost their mother, he wept briefly for us, but said he was sure that Kathleen would meet up with Sylvia and help to keep her company. There was a gentle earnestness in the way he spoke that soothed Tilde and Truman-Paul, and by the end of the meal even I had been moved to the point of almost believing that somewhere close by, just beyond grasp of our senses, his wife and Kathleen were there watching us and telling us to be strong and to carry on. I stopped short of agreeing to go with him to the chapel after we'd eaten, but I let him take the children while I went back out on the deck to talk to Trung.

Night was falling, bringing with it a resumption of the rain. Trung had left the lifeboat. As I was searching the ship for him, I ran into the newlyweds, who I hadn't seen in days. They were slightly drunk and in high spirits, and wondered if I could take a picture of them slow-dancing in the rain near the pool. I obliged them, and they proceeded to dance their way up to the diving board and out to its end, where they turned to offer me wide grins for posterity, then danced the ten foot drop into the water. Laughing and singing, they splashed their way to the shallow end, then clung together in embrace. I took a final shot and set the camera down, then walked off, seeking out the dry interior of the ship. I wondered in how many different places and positions they'd made love so far on the cruise. I hoped, for their sake, that they'd reach a ripe old age where they could look back and laugh at times like this.

Trung was in his room, with the door locked again. I pounded on it.

"Come on, Trung, let me in."

"I'm sleeping."

"No you aren't. Let me in. I want to talk to you."

"I don't feel like talking."

"I think you should. I think we both should."

"Go away."

"Don't shut yourself off like this, Trung. I'm worried about you."

"I can take care of myself!"

"Look, Trung, do I have to go and get another key and let myself in? Is that what I'm going to have to do?"

"Oh, man. . . ." His voice was sounding closer to the door. I heard the latch turn, then he opened the door and glared up at me. "How come you can't just leave me alone?"

"Can I come in?" I asked calmly.

"What for?"

"I want to know what's going on with you, that's what for. I want to understand how you're feeling, how you're—"

"I'm feeling shitty," he said curtly. "That good enough for you?"

"Trung. . . ."

"Look, I don't need to be babied."

I'd never seen him this worked up before. "I'm not trying to baby you, Trung. I just—"

"Give me some 'space,' " he said mockingly. "Just like you want at breakfast. Just give me a little space, okay?"

I backed away, holding my hands up like he had a gun on me. "Okay, Trung. If that's what you want, you got it. I don't want to fight with you."

"Don't worry," he said, calming down slightly. "I'll be better in the morning."

"Whatever you say, Trung."

He closed the door and threw the lock again. I shook my head to myself, frustrated that I couldn't communicate with him. I didn't have much time to dwell on it, though, because Truman-Paul and Tilde were coming down the corridor towards me.

"Mr. Peachum's such a sweet man," Tilde was saying.

"We got to put a quarter in a coin box and then lit a candle for mom!" Truman-Paul said excitedly. "Mr. Peachum said it was kind of like using a telephone, only you were calling somebody in the 'spearchal' world."

"He just meant it symbolically, Truman-Paul," Tilde said. She told me, "We traded addresses so we can keep in touch after the trip."

"That's nice."

"He said he talked to you before and that you're a good person," Truman-Paul boasted.

I grinned, ruffling his hair. "You mean he had to *tell* you that?"

"No, but. . . ."

I knelt down and hugged them both. "Well, I'm glad you went and had a good time. Now, I don't know about you, but I'm ready for some sleep."

"Are we going to be back on land tomorrow?" Truman-Paul asked.

I nodded. "We should be in Tunis by morning."

"Tunis? Where's that?"

"That's where they make tuna fish, Truman-Paul," I said.

"Hah!" he laughed at me. "I *bet*!"

"How much?" I said, winking at Tilde.

Truman-Paul looked at his sister. She shrugged her shoulders, then giggled slightly. Truman laughed and pointed at me, "Yeah, you're kidding!"

"We'll see," I said, opening their door for them. "For now, though, it's bed time."

"I'm not tired."

"Then count sheep," I suggested, smiling. "Or fish."

They each leaned up for a goodnight kiss, then I closed the door on them and went into my room, feeling a little better. I was still worried about Trung, but after giving it a lot of thought I decided he was just acting his age and that the best thing I could do was give him room to grow.

An hour passed and I was still tossing in bed despite my fatigue. I turned on the lamp over the headboard and leaned across the floor, snatching my wallet from the rear pocket of my pants. I took out the Christmas picture I'd looked at on the plane, days before. The kids had grown even more than I'd imagined then. I dwelled on the image of Kathleen and Mitchell, standing side-by-side, his arm around her, both of them staring outward with proud contentment. Maybe I should show the picture to Marie, I thought to myself. Maybe it would help her to understand why I was giving the children up. Or would it? I put a thumb over Mitchell's face and imagined my grinning mug there instead, then covered up Kathleen so that it was just me and the kids. Merry Christmas, from the four of us to all of you. Seasons Greetings from the Tannens. Postmark, Malibu, California. . . .

I heard a sudden scream from the children's room. It was Truman-Paul. I bolted from the bed and threw on my housecoat on the way out the door. The scream ended as quickly as it had sounded, and when I burst into the room, Tilde was sitting on the bed next to Truman-Paul, running her fingers through his hair as he stirred slightly under the covers. She put a finger to her lips before I could say anything.

"He'll be okay," she said softly, looking down at her fingers. "He was just having a nightmare. This helps make it go away."

I came over and knelt by the side of the bed, remembering something Mitchell had said about Truman's dreaming the first day we came aboard the ship.

Once she was sure Truman-Paul had fallen back asleep, she looked at me. Her eyes were moist and her voice had a tenderness that made my heart ache. "He dreams about a white kangaroo," she spoke in a broken whisper. "It has long fingernails and whiskers that are stiff and sharp, like needles . . . and long teeth. It has a dead baby in its pouch . . . and it chases him." A single tear rolled down her face. "Isn't that awful? That he has to suffer like that?" She looked at him protectively. "You'd think he'd at least be allowed to feel safe in his sleep."

I stared at them, in awe that I had had a part in the creation of two beings so incredibly loveable. It wasn't only Kathleen that I could see in them now. I realized that I was there, too, filled with promise and potential, another chance for decency and innocence to make a difference in the world.

"He's very lucky to have you, Tilde," I whispered once I found the courage to speak.

"He needs me, especially now," she said, sounding like someone twice her age. "I like to take care of him."

I looked into her eyes, seeing the child lurking behind her stoic front. "And who takes care of you, Tilde?"

She remained still, the only motion being the slow movement of her fingers through Truman-Paul's hair. Then I could detect a quivering of her lower lip, and soon the slight trembling spread out to the rest of her. I opened my arms to her and she lunged into my embrace, crying, "Oh, Daddy. Oh, Daddy!" She said it over and over again as I held her tightly, feeling her warm tears against my neck.

"Oh, Daddy!"

Two short words. I'd never heard better ones in my life.

CHAPTER TWENTY-EIGHT

I stayed with them in their room that night. By morning we were moored in Tunis and there was sunshine pouring through the window. Tilde was fast asleep beside me, and Truman-Paul was snoring in his bed across from us. I got up carefully so as not to wake them and went to the window. We were a few hundred yards out from shore, where the tops of mosques and spires of old buildings shared the skyline with rising rectangles of modern highrises. It was the one port-of-call on our itinerary I'd never been to, and in a way I was looking forward to it. It would be a place without memories to contend with, a place to go to and get caught up in the thrill of newfound discoveries.

"Mornin', Dad," Truman-Paul yawned, sitting up in bed and stretching.

"How you doing, T.P.?" I whispered, coming over and hugging him. "Get a good night's sleep?"

He nodded. "Dad, what's a tuna fish look like?"

"If we spot one today, I'll point it out for you, okay?"

"Come on. . . ." he said.

Tilde was stirring now. I checked my watch and said, "We're only going to be here half a day, so I want to get an early start. Why don't you and your sister get ready

192

and we'll have a nice, full breakfast so we have plenty of energy." I leaned over and kissed Tilde. "Mornin', doll."

She smiled and I left them. Before going into my room, I tried Trung's door. It wasn't locked. I knocked.

"Good morning, Trung. Can I come in?"

There was no answer. I opened the door and peered in.

"What the. . . ."

The room was a mess, but not so much because Trung had things lying around. Drawers and closet doors were pulled open, hangers lay strewn on the floor with travel brochures, and the blankets lay in a heap at the floor of the bed.

Trung's things were gone. So was Trung.

"Shit!" I spun around and rushed down the hallway, almost bowling over the Hungarian brothers as I rounded the corner, looking wildly about for Trung. Spotting a steward leaving one of the other cabins with a breakfast cart, I hurriedly came over.

"Excuse me, but have you seen my son?" I asked him. "He's the Filipino, dark hair, about five foot six and—"

"He's gone ashore," the steward told me calmly.

"What?"

"Yes, sir. On the first launch this morning."

"I don't believe it!" I ranted. "You just let him go? He's just a kid, for Christ's sake. Don't you people—"

"Sir, the launch is available for all passengers to take ashore as they please," the steward told me stuffily. "It's not for us to play the part of nannies or man-servants."

I would love to have throttled him, or at least yanked his nose so it wasn't stuck in the air so haughtily, but I didn't have the time or nerve. Instead, I asked him irritably, "When's the next boat going ashore?"

"There's always a launch going back and forth. If there's not one waiting now, it should be along shortly. Now, if you'll excuse me. . . ." He started to roll his cart off, then, as an afterthought, or maybe to placate his guilt, he added, "Oh, he *did* ask for directions to the market."

I slammed a fist into my palm, swearing, "Son of a bitch!" Why hadn't I seen it coming? Was I *that* blind?

I changed quickly and made sure Tilde and Truman-Paul were dressed appropriately for a search party, then we made our way to the lower deck, joining up with the older married couple we'd run across several times on the ship—the pair who were happiest when they were at each other's throats. The five of us filled up the launch enough to merit a run to shore. The waters of the harbor were calm and we made good time. The oldlyweds kept things interesting on the way with their bickering over use of the camera.

"You *know* I hate it when you use the wide-angle lens, so why do you always insist on taking it?" she complained.

"Because there's some shots when I *need* a wide-angle lens, dearie, that's why."

"But it always makes me look so fat. . . ."

"Then stay out of the picture when I'm using it. When I'm using it, I'm trying to take in a large area, and I'm not talking about your rearend, either."

"Arthur! Watch what you say. There's children here."

"I see, I see. Cute little buggers, too. Hey, mister, mind if I take a picture of your kids with the shoreline in the background?"

"What about me, Arthur? Why don't you take a shot of *me* with the shoreline in the background?"

"Because I'm using the wide-angle lens, sweetheart, remember? Okay, kids, say 'cheeeese'!"

Once we reached the docks, we got into the first cab with a driver that spoke English and had him take us to the market district. We rode deeper into the older section of town, the Tunis of dirt roads and sandalled feet, of men in robes and women with twig-framed crates balanced on their heads, of bleating goats and prancing chickens roaming freely in search of food. We'd find Trung here if we were going to find him anywhere.

"Why'd he run away?" Truman-Paul wanted to know as we got out of the taxi to begin covering ground on foot.

"We'll have to ask him that when we find him," I said, looking furtively around.

"*If* we find him," Tilde said less optimistically. "There must be a million people here!"

"But only one Trung. We can't give up."

We called out his name as we edged our way through the clotted masses congregating in various market squares, but our cries were lost in the cacaphony and we finally stopped, deciding that if he *did* hear us he might run off before we could spot him. It was a hot day, and by noon we were sweating and exhausted, with nothing to show for our efforts. Our ship would be pulling anchor to start its crossing to Genoa in a few hours.

"I'm getting blisters on my toes," Truman-Paul complained. "Can we stop and rest?"

"A little longer," I urged, glancing down alleyways and into the shadowed recesses of doorways. There were plenty of boys there, younger than Trung, hunger in their eyes and hearts. Why did he want to return to that life?

"Maybe he's already gone back to the ship," Tilde suggested hopefully. "Maybe he just came ashore to get a surprise gift or something."

"He wouldn't have packed all his things and taken them with him if he planned on coming back," I said. "No, he's still here. We'll look another—"

"Dad. . . ." Truman-Paul hissed, tugging at my shirt as he pointed down the street.

I looked and saw Trung standing in front of a Tunisian peddler who was looking over his portable video game. Behind the peddler was a cart filled with trinkets.

Motioning for Tilde and Truman-Paul to keep quiet, I led them down the dirt roadway, veering to keep the crowd between us and Trung. He didn't notice me until I was reaching out to grab him.

"Trung," I exclaimed, overjoyed at finding him.

"No!" he shouted, wrenching himself free of my grip and pushing his way through the throng. I took up the chase, with Tilde and Truman-Paul right behind me. Trung was running as if possessed, twisting his body with uncanny finesse to avoid collisions with pedestrians moving too slow to get out of his way. One old woman in battered robes moved the wrong way and Trung overturned a cart filled with pottery vases trying to get around her. It slowed him down momentarily, but not enough for me to catch up with him. I didn't manage that until we'd run out of crowds for him to maneuver through and I could gain ground on a deserted side street. I overtook him as we were passing an archway that led into an open courtyard, and I dragged him inside, slamming him hard against a pillar in the center of the clearing.

"What the hell do you think you're doing?!!" I gasped as we wrestled. "You're in Africa, you stupid son-of-a-bitch! This isn't your home, or even—"

"Leave me alone!" Trung shouted, kicking at me, tears of rage and anger coming to his eyes. "Let me go!"

I pinned him against the wall, just as mad as he was. "Look, you want the crap knocked out of you? That's what'll happen to you here. Try to pawn your shirt and they'll slit your throat to pay you for it! They play for keeps here, Trung! Do you hear me?"

"What do you care?" he bawled, putting up the last of his struggling. "You don't want me, so just let me go! I can take care of myself!"

I shook my head as I held him in place. Behind me, I heard Tilde and Truman-Paul rushing into the courtyard, whispering excitedly to one another.

"What do you want from me?!" Trung snarled through his teeth, still squirming to get free. "Let me go!"

"No!" I shouted.

"What's the difference? You don't want me!"

So that was it, I realized. I shook him slightly. "That's not true, Trung. . . ."

"You don't want to be with me . . . !" he wailed miserably, no longer resisting.

I let him go, but kept myself between him and the archway leading from the courtyard. "It has nothing to do with wanting!" I told him.

"Just let me go. Forget about me."

"No way," I told him firmly. "I won't do that."

"You don't want to be with me!" he repeated stubbornly.

"There are things here you're not aware of, Trung."

"You don't *want* me!"

"It has nothing to do with wanting!" I said between breaths, trying to make him understand. "There's a big difference between wanting and being *able*!" I could see that the others were listening to, so I tried to make it as clear to all of them as I could. "I can't give you the things Mitchell can give you. Can't you see that? It's not that I don't *want* to. It's that I *can't*."

Truman-Paul was listening, all right. He stepped forward and shouted, "*Can't* means *won't*! You said so!" I turned around, surprised by the sudden anger in his eyes. "That's what you told me! If you really wanted to do something, you could do it!"

"Well, maybe I was wrong!" I said, disheartened. "Maybe I didn't understand your situation, Truman. Maybe I didn't respect you enough to know that you really *were* trying, as hard as you could. Maybe wanting isn't enough after all."

I couldn't tell from Truman-Paul's expression whether he was unconvinced or feeling betrayed. Tilde was watching me with anguish, ready to cry. I turned back to Trung, determined to make my point.

"Are you unhappy living with Mitchell? You tell me there's something wrong with the way he treats you,

and I'll claim you right here on the spot." I pointed a
finger at him, daring him. "Now, you tell me the truth."

Trung glared back at me as if he were fed up with my
stupidity. "Mitchell inherited me," he said harshly. "My
own father left me. You're the only one who ever *chose*
me." I opened my mouth to say something, I don't
know what, but he kept shouting, "And don't tell me
you're not my father . . . you say you're just my 'friend'.
You think I let you adopt me because I wanted a
'friend'?" He spat at my feet with contempt.

"Trung," I said lamely, "I . . ."

"I don't need friends like you," he sobbed, buckling
at the knees with emotion. "I need fathers like you!"

I rushed forward and caught him, put my arms around
him. Tilde and Truman-Paul moved in to be close to
us. Their eyes were all on me, waiting for me to say
something.

"Okay . . . okay," I said, soothing Trung by stroking his back. "Easy now, easy. We're just upset now
. . . but we're going to get through this . . . we're
going to get used to all this and move on. We're going to
make it." I glanced at Tilde and Truman-Paul and said,
with more conviction, "We are."

CHAPTER TWENTY-NINE

We were together on the deck that night as the ship pulled out of the harbor and set its course for Genoa. A boisterous party was taking place around the pool nearby, and we mingled idly with those passengers celebrating on this, their last night aboard the ship. After the monstrous dinner we'd just finished indulging ourselves in, it was hard to watch people lined up for a limbo contest, shaking back and forth as they leaned backwards and tried to wriggle under a bamboo pole raised only a couple feet off the ground.

"Any of you guys want to try that?" I asked the kids.

Truman-Paul seemed ready to try. Standing next to me, he started shaking his arms and arching his back, giggling, "Like this?"

"Hey, man," Trung teased. "You're so short you don't even need to lean back."

Truman-Paul made a face at Trung. "Very funny."

I gave Trung a nudge, taunting, "Hey, you're such an expert, why don't you show us how it's done?"

"Yeah!" Truman-Paul chanted gleefully.

"Yeah, Trung," Tilde added.

Trung glanced over, watching the Hungarian twins passing under the poles from both directions, doing a crab walk and earning a round of laughter from those gathered around them.

"They're just clowning around, Trung," I said. "To do it right you can't use your hands."

"I know *that*," Trung complained. He contemplated the pole a while longer, then shook his head, rubbing his stomach. "If I didn't just have supper, it'd be a piece of cake."

"Your supper *was* a piece of cake, Trung." I grinned at him. "Try a better excuse."

"Okay, you suckers!" he said, rubbing his hands together. "You think I'm bluffing? You'll see."

There was a pause while the newlyweds had their fun, with the wife taking a picture of her husband pretending to do the high jump over the bar in slow motion. He knocked the pole off its stand when he was getting up for a bow. Trung moved in and lowered the pegs on the stand so that when he set the pole down, there was only about twenty inches of clearance. He stepped back and concentrated on the pole as the band in the background gave him a drum roll. Trung started towards the pole, bending at the knees, swaying from side to side as he lowered himself further and further, holding his arms out to keep his balance. The murmurs amongst the crowd changed to gasps and a burst of applause as Trung passed neatly under the pole, missing it with more than an inch to spare.

"Trung!" Truman-Paul shouted. "You did it!"

Beaming, Trung stood up and bowed to the crowd, loving the attention. I watched him with both pride and sadness, and when our eyes met, I saw a glimpse of the maturity he would be reaching for throughout the rest of his adolescence. This was more than mere showing off for him. I'd seen him in limbo contests on the streets of Manila, earning pesoes from tourists as just one of his schemes for surviving without a home. He was telling me he would have managed to get by in Tunis if we hadn't found him. He'd come back with us because he wanted to, not because he felt he had to.

"Congratulations, Trung," I told him, holding my palm out.

He slapped it, then I gave him five back. He laughed, "You're lucky I didn't ask for bets."

On our way back to our rooms, I suggested we all bunk together in my cabin for the night. We could haul in extra mattresses and camp out on the floor.

"Oh boy!" Truman-Paul voted. "Yeah!"

"That sounds like fun," Tilde seconded.

I looked over at Trung. "Well, what do you say? It's gotta be unanimous."

"What are we going to *do*?" he said sarcastically. "Sit around a fire and sing songs or something?"

"Why, that's a great idea, Trung!" I said, "That's just what we'll do."

Trung rolled his eyes. "You gotta be kidding, man!"

"Look, if I can make a campfire in my room, will you promise to stay there and sing the hokiest camp songs you know?"

He looked at me suspiciously. "What are you going to do, flick your Bic or something?"

"No cheap tricks," I promised. "These will be genuine special effects."

Trung thought it over, then nodded. "Okay. You got a deal."

We shook on it, then I sent them back with the keys to set up the room while I tracked down a few supplies I'd need. When I got back to my cabin a while later, there were four mattresses crowding the floor, with a four-foot-wide space in the middle for the 'campfire'. I sent them out of the room while I set things up, then made them promise to close their eyes when they came back in and sat down.

"Now, keep them shut until I say it's okay to open them," I said, flicking off the lights and unplugging the smoke alarm. I lighted a match and held the flame under a plastic bag I'd hung from the ceiling by a piece of wire. As soon as the bag caught fire, it began to drip hot dollops of shriveled plastic, which warbled like science-fiction sound effects as they fell into a bucket of water set in the clearing, then sizzled out.

"Now."

The kids opened their eyes and watched the steady stream of glowing blobs falling noisily into the bucket.

"Wow!" Truman-Paul exclaimed. "Neat!"

"Where'd you learn how to do that?" Tilde asked, amazed.

"College."

The show didn't last for long. When it was over, I sat down with the kids, leaving the lights off. There was plenty of moonlight pouring into the room.

"Well, Trung," I whispered.

"I don't know any camp songs."

"Baloney. You've been to camp the past four summers. Who do you think you're kidding?"

"But I never sang those stupid songs."

"Uh huh," Truman-Paul said. "I heard you."

"Gimme a break," Trung whined.

"You just start and we'll join in," Tilde bartered.

"A deal's a deal, Trung," I reminded him.

He groaned, then paused a moment before humming a few bars, then started to sing, "One hundred bottles of beer on the wall/One hundred bottles of beer/Take—"

"Trung. . . ."

He laughed, then began again. This time it was *Old MacDonald Had A Farm*, not much better but a move in the right direction. ". . . and on this farm he had a video game/Eeee-Eye-Eeee-Eye-oh/With a Pac-Man here/A Pac-Man there/Here a Pac/There a Man/Everywhere a Pac-Man . . ." We joined in. Tilde did a biochemist, I opted for a golf pro, and Truman-Paul, of course, thought the farm needed a tuna fish.

We went around in a circle, everybody taking turns leading another song. We did them all *John Jacob*

Jinkleheimer-Schmitt (or whatever his name was), *Kookaberra Sleeps in the Old Gum Tree, They're Be a Hot Time in the Old Town Tonight.* It had been more than twenty-five years since I'd been to camp, and in all honesty I'd thought I'd never again be able to sing those old songs with any semblance of sincerity or feeling. Especially *'Kumbaya.'* But by the time two hours had passed and the three had fallen asleep around me, I sang *Kumbaya* softly to myself and felt the same gnawing heartache I'd felt the last night of any stay at camp, when I'd come to the realization that the magically special times of the past few days were drawing to a close and that the next day I'd be on my way back home alone, leaving the others behind.

CHAPTER THIRTY

Knuckles rapped on the cabin door, followed by a voice from the hallway. I was only half-awake and most of the message slipped past me. A few seconds later, I heard the steward knock on the door to Trung's room and repeat the announcement. "It's eight o'clock. We'll be arriving in Genoa in three hours. Please have your luggage ready to be taken ashore by noon."

Trung stirred on the mattress butting up against mine, and Tilde was across from me, yawning herself awake. I didn't see Truman-Paul. The bathroom door was wide open and he wasn't there, either. Crawling on all fours, I moved past the bucket filled with water and the floating globs of plastic that had provided last night's light show. I felt Truman-Paul's mattress. It was cold.

"Either of you guys see Truman-Paul get up during the night?"

Tilde shook her head.

"I was out cold," Trung said, pushing his bangs out of his face. "What was that guy saying?"

"He said we're in the homestretch, Trung. Three hours and we'll be in Genoa."

"I better get packed," Tilde said.

"I already am," Trung said. He and I looked at one another.

"I'm glad we found you yesterday, Trung. We'd still be in Tunis looking if we hadn't. You know that, don't you?"

He nodded, smiling tightly. "I'm glad you found me, too . . . Dad."

I put on my bathrobe and went out into the hallway. Mr. Peachum was down near the exit, talking with one of the stewards. We nodded greetings to each other, then I knocked on the door to Truman's room.

"Hey, Truman-Paul, you in there?"

"Just a minute," he said. ". . . Okay. You can come in now."

When I opened the door, he was standing in front of his bed, looking up at me strangely.

"What is it, Truman-Paul?" I asked. "You all right?"

He stepped to one side, giving me a view of the bed. The spelling blocks were strewn out across the bedspread like ruins in the wilderness, but he'd pulled some of the letters aside and lined them up in a neat row.

P–O–L–E–I–C–M–A–N.

"Is that right?" he asked me uncertainly.

If I had a cartoon jaw, it would have dropped to the floor, then bounced back and spread my grin out into something that would have made the Chesire Cat start thinking about another line of work. I looked at Truman-Paul proudly. "Well, it's damn close."

He scrunched his face up and it took me a second to realize that he was impersonating me giving him a lecture. "See what you can do when you really want to?" he said earnestly.

I came over and grabbed him under the arms, then lifted him up and hugged him. "I sure do, Truman-Paul," I told him. "I sure do."

Tilde came in and smiled when she saw the blocks set out on the bed. "Fantastic!"

"I did it," Truman-Paul boasted. "All by myself."

Tilde took the "E" block and shifted it into its proper place. "Only one letter off. Truman-Paul, that's just great!"

"I'll get even better!" he promised.

Tilde was going to start packing, but I suggested that we eat first. On our way to the dining room, we passed a lot of passengers who were already setting their luggage outside their doors for the porters to tend to. The Hungarian twins, identical in all they had done so far on this cruise, stepped out of character, revealing separate tastes in luggage. One was traveling in Samsonite, the other by footlocker and canvas tote bags. As we passed the room belonging to the newlyweds, we heard sniffling inside and glanced in to see the wife sitting by the side of her bed with an unwrapped present in her lap and her husband leaning over to kiss her on the cheek. He'd brought her a photo album.

The dining room was the least crowded I remembered seeing it. The only other people sitting near our table were the middle-aged couple who'd sustained themselves thus far with their constant bickering. This morning, however, they were eating quietly, lost in thought. When they looked up at each other from time to time, they smiled, no doubt reflecting on the grand times they'd shared.

Our meals were being served when I saw Marie come in. She looked our way and smiled. I waved her over.

"Well," she said when she'd joined us. "This is farewell. I was going to join you for the last breakfast, but I see your extra chair is gone."

"Yeah, well, they finally got around to taking it away," I said, starting to get up. "Look, I'll get another one—"

"No, no," Marie said. "I should really sit with my people, after all." She looked at the children, sensing something, then turned to me. "I'm not going to ask," she whispered delicately. "I'll just cross my fingers."

I stood up and embraced her, then forewarned the

kids, "Better watch out. I'm going to give this lady a kiss."

For such a short kiss, we managed to squeeze in a lot of feeling. I could only hope that when it was time for me to fall in love with another woman, she would be someone as caring as Marie.

"Goodbye," she told the children.

"Bye."

"Goodbye, Marie."

"We'll miss you."

She looked back to me. "Goodbye, James."

I nodded, not knowing what to say. She started off, then I called out, "Marie?"

She looked back.

"*Au revoir*."

She flashed a smile. "*Au revoir*."

Until we meet again.

I sat back down, telling the children, "There's goes one nice lady."

They nodded.

"A nice lady," Truman-Paul agreed between mouthfuls of scrambled eggs.

"What's Genoa like?" Trung asked.

"Well, it's the heart of the Italian Riviera," I said, still watching Marie cross the room. "You know about the Riviera, don't you?"

"Yeah," Trung grinned. "Lots of chicks."

"Don't be so crude," Tilde said. She asked me, "Doesn't it look a lot like where you live?"

"A little, I guess, Tilde."

"We'll like it, then," Truman-Paul said.

"You guys like California?" I asked them.

"It was fun," Truman-Paul insisted. "We had a blast!"

"Lots of chicks," Trung said, sneering at Tilde. "I mean 'women'."

"We've only been there *once*, Daddy," Tilde reminded me.

"Well, maybe you guys should spend a little more time there," I suggested.

"That'd be great," Trung said.

"Yeah!" Truman-Paul shouted.

"What do you mean?" Tilde asked me, trying to read my thoughts. "Do you mean like a longer vacation with you? Would we be going there after this?"

"I don't know," I said. "I'm still working on that." And I was working on it as fast as I could. It was already after nine. Genoa was only three hours away.

So was Mitchell.

CHAPTER THIRTY-ONE

There was a clifftop park overlooking the harbor in Genoa. The grounds were immaculately kept, from the thick carpet of weedless grass to the winding flowerbeds and well-spaced eucalyptus trees. Here and there was a statue that bore the wear of ages and stared out from its landscaped surroundings with a look of quiet contemplation. This was a haven of serenity and quiet, meant for idle strolls, leisure reading of good poetry or sketching of the myriad nature studies to be found wherever one looked.

I walked past a bed of small-bulbed roses and entered the clearing. I saw Mitchell standing by a railing that afforded a view of the coastline below. He was wearing his white suit again, and holding his Panama at his side.

"Mitchell," I called out as I strode up to him.

He turned around. There was an enigmatic expression on his face that changed only in degree when he saw that I was alone.

"You said you were bringing them," he said.

"They're right down there," I said, pointing past him to a spit of rocks stretching out into the harbor. The children were there, watching the activity at the docks and skipping stones out into the deep-blue water. "I wanted to talk to you first."

He stared down at the children a moment. When he looked at me, there was a sadness in his eyes I hadn't expected, hadn't accounted for. Maybe he saw it coming.

"I'm keeping them, Mitchell," I told him firmly.

He continued to look at me with that strange look in his eyes. I couldn't believe this was the same man who had bore into me with such angry menace in Cairo only a few days before. Perhaps he'd been troubled over the extent of his vindictiveness during that encounter.

Or maybe he'd been moved to see the situation through my eyes, much the way I'd come to grasp his relationship with the kids. Whatever the reason, it was clear that the fight was gone from Mitchell. He stood numbly as I rambled on, mouthing the argument I'd been piecing together since the moment I'd decided that, as Marie had told me, I was the children's father, that they were mine.

"You can take me to court," I told him. "I'm willing to do battle. I know in my heart I'll win."

His lips parted slightly, as if he were about to say something, but no words came forth. His eyes took on a glassy sheen and began to redden from the tears that were forming. Much as I'd braced myself for an anticipated showdown by trying to convince myself that Mitchell was an enemy, to be dealt with accordingly, I knew it was more complicated than that. A lot more complicated. He wanted what was best for them, and, if anything, I was proposing to usurp him as the one who would be in charge of seeing to those needs.

"You see, Mitchell," I said, trying to make him understand, perhaps trying to make sure I understood myself. "There's one thing we kept forgetting to consider, and that's what *they* wanted."

His fingers were curling around the rim of the Panama. He still refused to speak, and I could sense he wasn't preparing to strike back with another of his eloquent denunciations. I'm sure there'd been times in court when last-minute testimony or the arrival of certain evidence would suddenly undermine his whole case, and he would know the futility of pressing forward any further. That was the way he seemed now, and I felt obliged to follow through with what I'd started.

"Their teachers are Mr. Worsham, Mrs. Flaum, and Mr. McKee," I told him. "Tilde's best friend is named Sarah. Trung is sweet on a girl named Jennie. I've learned all this since Cairo . . . and that Truman-Paul dreams of a white kangaroo that's been chasing him for about four years now—the length of time I've been gone. I realize this doesn't make me an expert, but I'm ready to learn."

If there had been another way of handling this, I wished to hell I'd known about it, because as I stood there watching the first few tears steal down Mitchell's face, I felt a loathing at what I'd done. It didn't matter that he'd subjected me to the same treatment in Athens and Cairo. He'd been within his rights, perhaps even his duty, then, when my sense of adequacy as a parent had been, at best, delusionary. If anything, I owed him a debt of gratitude for the slap in the face his diatribes had given me. It had been him, along with Marie and the children themselves, who had helped me to realize the decision I had to make, the decision I'd so easily renigged on in the past. Mitchell wasn't the enemy. He never had been. It had always been myself that was to blame, me and my team of shouldered devils coaching me to always put myself first, no matter what the cost. Those devils were gone now, I hoped, and Mitchell had knocked at least one of them off my shoulders.

"The children. . . ." I told him, "They love you."

Mitchell finally spoke, like a man wounded. "I love *them*."

"Yeah," I said, my own voice cracking. "You and I got a lot in common."

I grinned awkwardly, thinking I was suddenly on the

verge of something, some way to salvage this in a way that would satisfy everyone. It was a flash, the kind of bursting hope that comes without the convenience of planned-out details. I tried to go with it, extending my hand to Mitchell, hoping we might shake on the start of a new, workable arrangement. He looked down at my hand, gathering his composure, then turned and walked away from me, going to the railing where he could look down at the children.

I came over and stood beside him. Together we watched the kids. Trung was still skipping stones while Truman-Paul watched on, counting skips. Tilde was crouched over nearby, observing something clinging to one of the rocks. Three children, slowly growing, coming to terms with the world around them, a world they'd have to face without the valued presence of Kathleen to guide them. Now it was up to Mitchell and me.

"Come on, Mitch," I said to him. "Let's do them some good."

I could see that he was still struggling over this newest disruption of his ordered world, and it occurred to me that perhaps he was as ripe for change as I was. And if there was one thing I could say of myself at the end of this long, grueling journey, it was that I had, truly, begun to change. With time and persistence, I could only improve more.

I draped one arm around Mitchell's shoulder, then pointed to Mitchell with my free hand as I shouted out to the kids, "Hey! Look who I found! Any of you know this guy?"

The kids looked up and spotted us. They waved and cried back as they scrambled across the rocks to the shore.

"Mitchell!"

"Hi, Mitchell!"

"It's good to see you!"

As the children raced to a winding path that led up to the park, Mitchell and I started off to meet them—we were walking side-by-side.